IELTS

一次就考到

雅思口說

總是自信答完且能舉一反三

Amanda Chou
◎ 著

7+

MP3

三大學習特色 迅速組織「抽象類」話題的應答句／補強「時態」表達／豐富且具體化個人「感受」和「經驗」的表達

掌握抽象類話題的變化：協助考生巧妙應對題型的轉變，在口說考試的三個PART突然遇到工作和金錢等類別的抽象類話題時，也能處變不驚，迅速接續答完。

修正時態的使用：收錄遠超過1000句各類話題表達，有效修正表達各情境時在「時態」和「語法」的使用。

提升個人感受和細節性話題的表達：廣泛納入常考話題之外的**「風俗民情」**和**「異國美食」**類別等個人感受的表達，靈活表達出獨一無二的體驗，讓考官印象深刻。

　　在雅思口說考試中，要獲取 6.5 分以上的成績，就是要學習更多道地語句和擺脫教科書式的口語表達。在近期的考題變化上，不難發現：其實考官更希望能看到的是**「個人化的特色表達」**、**「個人的感受和想法」**和**「更細節性的表達」**等。（表達的是否具體，一直是能否考到口說 7 分以上的關鍵。）

　　這部分牽涉到不僅在於語法上的正確性和道地英語的使用，而是需要有特定的情境或經驗作為輔助，才能更自然地表達出個人感受。這次書籍的規劃，大幅度增加了關於**「個人感受的表達語句」**，包含：到某知名景點品嚐道地美食，細節性描述其他層面，像是與其他人和動物的互動等等，例如：「遞棉花糖給浣熊，邊攝影牠們如何毀了棉花糖」或是「小心翼翼地示範如何用剪刀和鉗子開龍蝦殼，吃這道菜還真需要耐心和細心哩……」讓表達更真實（**genuine**）。（這部分是考官們更喜歡看到的！溝通，絕非是死板板的模板背誦。）

書籍中替考生篩選好了高分表達，考生可以在短時間內迅速學習吸收，在考試中 fake it，讓考官覺得你更不一樣，更能感受到你真正有這些體驗。（表達時的豐富程度和具體程度有關，而除了這兩項的強化外，在時態的使用上也會因為演練書中的語句而作出修正，一舉數得呀，畢竟許多考生有時候誤用現在完成式或忘記要用過去式的時態，在演練書中的表達句時，同步強化自身時態的使用。）

另外一個部分是考生確實演練了許多常考話題，例如「姓名」、「顏色」、「生日」、「音樂」等常考主題，但是很不巧，在考官話鋒轉問到了**較抽象**的話題時，考生就被考倒了（近期幾回劍橋雅思試題確實顯示口說考試的難度正在提升）。某部分原因是在亞洲國家更少關於像是金錢等方面的教育，考生要以英語表達出這些主題時會比較說不出個所以然，而在考試中被問到這些時，停頓太久或講話一直繞圈子就會被評定成 inability to talk about certain topics or redundant。**金錢類的妙答**則包含了像是「當然，答案是存下額外的錢。記得《巴比倫最富有的人》裡頭的古老智慧嗎？金錢來自於那些將它存下者。」有了這些**語料基礎**，更能於考試中發揮超乎水準的表現。

本書收錄了更多這些考生答不好的話題，提供考生在應考前做足準備。此外，確實在沒有太多工作經驗卻要講出與工作類相關的話題時，會相當吃力，有鑑於此，書中也納入了更多工作類和個人目標等的話題，每個表達句都以強化細節性表達和實際工作經驗作為基礎，例如：「我們還是需要這些配菜來完成整道主菜，因此我的動作被訓練得越來越快。舉涼拌捲心菜為例，我會用起司刨刀很快地削完一顆高麗菜，然後做出涼拌捲心菜來」，考生回應這類話題時，在表達方面更獨一無二且具體，有效補強某些考生在這幾個話題的弱項。

　　而如果是對話題卡題的人物類話題（像是描述一位名人）或對於科技（像是描述智慧型手機）和居住類（居住在城市好還是鄉下地區呢？）話題等較弱的考生，在書中也能找到實際的範例，提供考生能夠清楚且道地答好這類別的話題，一次考取高分！本書包含 74 個單元，提供考生能夠在最短時間內，海量練習且補強各類別話題的表達，絕對勝過課堂口說課，最後祝所有考生都能獲取理想成績。

倍斯特編輯部 敬上

使用說明 INSTRUCTIONS

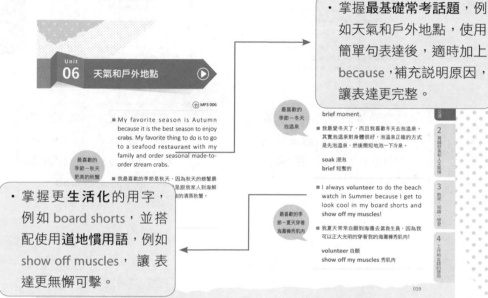

- 掌握最基礎常考話題，例如天氣和戶外地點，使用簡單句表達後，適時加上 because，補充説明原因，讓表達更完整。

Unit 06 天氣和戶外地點 ▶

MP3 006

最喜歡的一秋天把美的秋蟹

■ My favorite season is Autumn because it is the best season to enjoy crabs. My favorite thing to do is to go to a seafood restaurant with my family and order seasonal made-to-order stream crabs.

■ 我最喜歡的季節是秋天，因為秋天的螃蟹最肥美，最愛做的事就是跟我家人到海鮮餐廳點最新鮮現做的清蒸秋蟹。

- 掌握更生活化的用字，例如 board shorts，並搭配使用道地慣用語，例如 show off muscles，讓表達更無懈可擊。

最喜歡的季節一夏天泡溫泉

brief moment.

■ 我最愛冬天了，而且我喜歡冬天去泡溫泉。其實泡溫泉對身體很好，泡溫泉正確的方式是先泡溫泉，然後簡短泡一下冷泉。

soak 浸泡
brief 短暫的

■ I always volunteer to do the beach watch in Summer because I get to look cool in my board shorts and show off my muscles!

最喜歡的季節一夏天穿著海灘褲秀肌肉

■ 我夏天常自願到海邊去當救生員，因為我可以正大光明的穿著我的海灘褲秀肌肉！

volunteer 自願
show off my muscles 秀肌肉

039

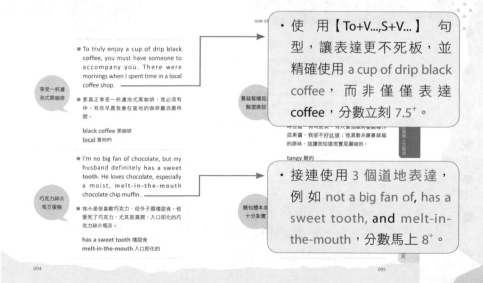

Unit 19

■ To truly enjoy a cup of drip black coffee, you must have someone to accompany you. There were mornings when I spent time in a local coffee shop.

享受一杯濾泡式黑咖啡

■ 要真正享受一杯濾泡式黑咖啡，我必須有伴。有些早晨我會在當地的咖啡廳消磨時間。

black coffee 黑咖啡
local 當地的

- 使用【To+V...,S+V...】句型，讓表達更不死板，並精確使用 a cup of drip black coffee，而非僅僅表達 coffee，分數立刻 7.5⁺。

蔓越莓嚐起來酸澀微甜

呀百甜一杯也可笑，有大直加糖的愛嬌爾作成果醬，我卻不好此道；我喜歡品嚐慕絲絲的原味，這讓我知道現實是嚴峻的。

tangy 酸的

■ I'm no big fan of chocolate, but my husband definitely has a sweet tooth. He loves chocolate, especially a moist, melt-in-the-mouth chocolate chip muffin.

巧克力碎片瑪芬蛋糕

■ 我不是很喜歡巧克力，但外子顯嗜甜食。他愛死了巧克力，尤其是濕潤、入口即化的巧克力碎片瑪芬。

has a sweet tooth 嗜甜食
melt-in-the-mouth 入口即化的

- 接連使用 3 個道地表達，例如 not a big fan of, has a sweet tooth, and melt-in-the-mouth，分數馬上 8⁺。

麵包體本身十分紮實

094

095

Unit 26 青木瓜沙拉上的蟹腳、冰火菠蘿油上的奶油魅力

▶ MP3 026

■ The **crushed** crab in our salad made Dan and I scared. Language barriers in Thailand mattered. Dan and I met in the **hostel** the first night I arrived in Bangkok.

沙拉中搗碎的螃蟹

■ 我們沙拉中搗碎的螃蟹使我和丹飽受驚嚇。在泰國這裡語言障礙真的有影響。丹和我是在我抵達曼谷的第一晚，在青年旅社認識的。

crushed 搗碎的

> · 注意時態的使用，描述曼谷的事情時，是過去發生的狀態，務必要使用**過去式**。

120

■ However, our biggest crises happened the very next day: this dish of green papaya salad in front of us. I could still see the uncrushed leg of crab with its fur on it.

面前這盤青木瓜沙拉

■ 然而，巨大的危機第二天就發生了，也就是我們面前這盤青木瓜沙拉。我還看得到一隻沒被搗碎的蟹腳耶。

crises 危機

■ Was it raw or cooked? We had no **clue**. Yet, to my surprise, Dan moved **forward** and took a bite. "If I'm poisoned, at least I saved your life." He joked.

蟹腳上還有毛

> · 在描述青木瓜沙拉時，具體表達出 the uncrushed leg of crab with its fur on it，而非僅講述 crab。

Unit 44 美國可拿滋、美國杯子蛋糕、法國蛙腿

▶ MP3 044

■ I visited Dominique Ansel's bakery in New York, of course, and got the real deal. Although the fake ones are everywhere, it is not **comparable** to the real thing! Here is my cronut experience: crispy, delicate, and beautiful.

享用真正道地的可拿滋

■ 我造訪了位在紐約的多明尼克．安西烘焙坊，並享用真正道地的可拿滋。雖然仿冒的可拿滋隨處可得，但那跟真貨可沒得比。如果你想要好味道，可得尋本溯源，對吧？我的可拿滋經驗如下：酥脆、精緻、美麗。

comparable 可比較的

> · 使用更口語化的 go up to，且運用價差比較出所想選的食物為何。

192

> · 描述完一段敘述後使用 3 個形容詞，簡潔且輕快傳達意思，讓表達不像死板板的背誦文。

去 Mister Donut 買可拿滋

guess.

■ 我都是去 Mister Donut 買可拿滋，他們做得不錯。唯一的缺點是，有時候麵翻不易掌控，結果弄得油膩膩。這要看糕餅師的技術和運氣了，我想。

greasy 油膩膩的

■ A cupcake can **go up to** $4 and that's like a burger in McDonald's. Instead of fancy yet **sugary** cakes, I'd rather go for savory sandwiches.

等於麥當勞一個漢堡

■ 一杯子蛋糕可達售價四美元，等於麥當勞一漢堡。要吃個漂亮但膩人的蛋糕，我寧願選正餐三明治。

go up to 可達
sugary 膩人的

193

Unit 58　個人特質: 描述對一個人來說最重要的特質

🎧 MP3 058

最重要的特質－高度動機 ❶

■ The most important quality is to be highly motivated. Remember that's the criteria that HR people use to assess a person's ability in the workplace. it's not just your intelligence or your ability.

■ 最重要的特質是有高度動機。記得人事部的人在評估一個人在工作場所能力的標準嗎？不僅僅是你的智力或你的能力。

criteria 標準
assess 評估

最重要的特質－高度動機 ❷

■ It's your motivation to the job and your ability. You multiply one's motivation and one's ability, and then you get what a person will bring to the company.

■ 是關於你對這份工作的動機和你的能力。你將一個人的動機乘上一個人的能力，然後你就可以得知這個人會替公司帶來什麼效益。

motivation 動機
multiply 乘上

・運用**具體實例**和**經驗**，而非含糊表達，例如人事部評估人的標準和動機乘上一個人的能力才是一個員工對公司的貢獻度。

...ted person will ...form those who ...telligence and ...little motivation.

表現超越那些僅仰賴...卻有著些許動機者。

欣賞的名人－Tyra Banks ❷

■ People are in desperate need of an inner compass because they can be so lost sometimes. Sometimes what she says can actually lead people to think in a certain direction.

■ 人們迫切需要心理內部的指南針，因為他們可能在有些時候感到迷失。有時候她所說的話實際上可以將人們導向以某個特定方向思考。

compass 指南針

・使用**慣用語**，像是 inner compass 等更道地且心靈雞湯式的用語，拉近與聆聽者的距離。

memoir 回憶錄

欣賞的作家－Ray Kroc ❶

■ Ray Kroc, the person who built the McDonald's empire, is the person I admire. He is an icon with traditional values and wisdom for later generations to learn from.

■ 雷‧克洛克，一位建造麥當勞帝國的人，是我所欽佩的對象。他是指標性人物，有著傳統價值和智慧讓較後面世代們可以從中學習到很多。

traditional 傳統的

・口語表達中，適時的使用同位語，補充說明人物或專有名詞，讓表達更清楚。

no age limits 年齡限制的
determination 決心

Unit 62

- 運用更**高階**的句型表達，例如 people within your circle，且適時運用**承轉詞** however 等字，讓表達更完善。

交友－結交各類型的朋友❷

■ People within your circle; however, often can only have **emotional support**, but **have nothing to offer**.

■ 人們自己的圈子裡呀，然而，通常只有著情感支持，但是卻沒什麼能幫上忙的。

emotional support 情感支持
have nothing to offer 沒什麼能幫上忙的

交友－結交各類型的朋友❶

■ You get to learn from different kinds of friends even though you have to do the **superficial** stuff. You just don't know how sometimes a **nodding acquaintance** can be quite helpful if you are out there looking for your ideal jobs.

■ 你能從不同類型的朋友中學習，即使你必須要做些些表面功夫。你不知道有時候就是這樣的點頭之交，在你想要找你的理想工作時發揮相當大的功用。

superficial 表面的
a nodding acquaintance 點頭之交

■ A person I know from the party once **introduced** me to the industry I've been longing to get into. I eventually get the job even though I have no experiences. From that moment on, I'm sort of like **what the heck**, the more the merrier.

交友－結交各類型的朋友

- 運用**常見慣用語**，例如 a nodding of acquaintance 和高階字彙 superficial，讓表達迅速拉高到 7 分的表達水平。

1 生活、娛樂、科技和交通
2 異國飲食和人文風情
3 教育、知識、學習

Unit 64

- 心機式的表達，表明總是從銷路最好的料理開始介紹。

🔊 MP3 064

介紹餐點－從銷路最好的

■ The priority does matter. Since there are many items on the menu, it's impossible to introduce every dish, which means that we have to **omit** some items in the introduction. I often start from our best-sellers.

■ 順序當然有影響，因為菜單上品項很多，不可能一一介紹，因此有些菜不會被介紹到。我總是從銷路最好的料理開始介紹。

omit 遺漏掉

介紹餐點－主餐收益較高

■ I always start from the entrées. Not only that it's more **profit** for us, but also every dish is my pride and joy. **Appetizers** and desserts have their reason to exist, but they are not my focus.

■ 我總是先從主餐開始介紹。不只是因為主餐收益較高，也因為每道菜都是我的驕傲。開胃菜和甜點當然也有存在的必要，但並非我的重點。

profit 利潤
appetizers 開胃菜

■ You will need a note pad with you while taking orders. For instance, if someone wants **meatloaf** without **ketchup** and another wants extra caramelized onions, things might get confused easily.

點餐－需要一本小記事本

點餐－

- 運用工作經驗實例，強化抽象類主題的答題。

277

1 生活、娛樂、科技和交通
2 異國飲食和人文風情
3 教育、知識、學習
4

- 使用更**具體**和**自然**的表達，例如在提到 side dishes 時，更明確列舉出了 baby spinach 和 coleslaw，讓考官知道你真的懂這些，這些來自於你的**實際工作體驗**。

食材用完－
常發生配菜不足

■ Quite frequently, what we run out of are the **side dishes**. Bok choy, **baby spinach**, coleslaw, etc.

■ 很常發生配菜不足的情況，例如青江菜、幼菠菜葉或涼拌捲心菜等。

side dishes 配菜
baby spinach 幼菠菜葉

pleasant 令人愉悅的
satisfaction 滿意

■ I'm not the one that makes the food, so I'm probably not that **annoyed**. However, I'm not **thrilled** to pass on this message to the kitchen.

■ 我不是煮飯的那個人，所以被惹惱的程度比較低。不過，要把這類訊息傳達給廚房，我

更換餐點－
惹惱的程度較低

- 適時運用**對等連接詞**，例如 so 等連接兩個句子，讓表達更完整。

食材用完－
用起司刨刀

■ We still need them to accomplish our main course, so I'm trained to move very fast. Take **coleslaw** for example, I'll use a cheese grater to quickly **shave up** a cabbage and whip it up.

■ 我們還是需要這些配菜來完成整道主菜，因此我的動作被訓練得越來越快。舉涼拌捲心菜為例，我會用起司刨刀很快地削完一顆高麗菜，然後做出涼拌捲心菜來。

coleslaw 涼拌捲心菜
shave up 削（蔬菜）

1 生活、娛樂、科技和交通
2 �腦飲食和人文風情
3 教育、知識、學習
4 工作和金錢的使用

■ Often you can **blow** the chance for your desired job and **regret** from ten years on that I wish I had prepared those questions.

■ 通常你會搞砸你想要的工作機會，而十年後後悔著但願我當時有準備那些問題。

求職面試－
Knock'em
Dead ❷

blow 搞砸
regret 後悔

- 使用**道地慣用語**，像是 blow the chance 並且多注意像 wish 這類常在生活中使用的表達，避免犯常見文法錯誤。

confident 自信的
whether 是否

■ Good **eye contact**. Definitely the most important one. Most of **human interactions** rest on good eye contact.

■ 良好的眼神接觸。絕對是最重要的一個。大多數人類互動是仰賴良好的眼神接觸。

求職面試－
眼神接觸 ❶

eye contact 眼神接觸
human interactions 人類互動

■ Or whether you are telling them the truth, and sometimes trust comes from having good eye contact. From my experience as an HR **manager**, interviewees who maintain good eye contact generally leave a good

- 使用更高階且訊息完整的描述，像是 most of human interactions rest on good eye contact，讓自己迅速脫穎而出。

2 貢腦飲食和人文風情
3 教育、知

目次 CONTENTS

Part 1 一般常見主題：生活、娛樂、科技和交通

**Part 2 個人感受、經驗和細節：
異國飲食和人文風情**

Part 3 抽象類話題 ❶：教育、知識、學習

Part 4 抽象類話題 ❷：工作和金錢的使用

Part 1 精選了比較特別的主題（畢竟考生都很熟悉像是取名字或顏色等相關的基礎話題了），這些精選的主題在考試中的 3 個 part 都很常詢問到，快來練習吧！

Part

1

一般常見主題：
生活、娛樂、
科技和交通

生活方式：
談論生活模式的改變

MP3 001

生活方式
改變－
現今科技

■ People nowadays have so many options in life and they tend to **make a comparison** with others, whether it is the figures or **appearances**. They have current technologies to help them get there.

■ 人們現今在生活中有許多選擇而他們傾向與他人做比較，不論是在體態或外表上。他們有著現今的科技幫助他們達到結果。

make a comparison 做比較
appearance 外表

■ They want to look good on the outside so that they **calculate** every calorie they **consume**. Girls eat only vegetables and fruits with less sugars at night. They do the mini plastics to remove fats in their body.

生活方式改變－飲食攝取

■ 他們想要在外在上看起來好看，所以他們就會計算每項他們所攝取的卡路里。女孩在晚間只吃蔬菜和糖分較少的水果。他們作微整形手術移除他們體內的脂肪。

calculate 計算
consume 攝取

■ People nowadays have **bombarded** messages from TVs, Videos on **platforms**, such as You tube and Facebook.

生活方式改變－轟炸式訊息

■ 人們現今從電視、平台上的視頻，例如 youtube 和臉書，有著轟炸式的訊息。

bombarded 轟炸式的
platform 平台

生活方式
改變－新聞
報導的提醒

■ News reports inform us of **repercussions** of eating in a certain way, and people who watch news reports about chronic illnesses and cancers are the result of unhealthy lifestyles will deep down have a warning label inside to not choose unhealthy foods.

■ 新聞報導告知我們以特定方式的飲食習慣會帶來的後果，而且人們觀看關於慢性病和癌症的新聞報導是不健康的生活型態的結果，這將在內心深處有著警告的標誌留下，提醒你別選擇不健康的食物。

repercussion 後果

生活方式
改變－專家
教育和提醒

■ TV programs invite doctors and health **specialists** educating people how to eat healthy. These channels are what people in the past didn't have.

■ 電視節目邀請醫生和健康專家教育人們如何吃的健康。這些頻道是人們過去所沒有的。

specialists 專家

■ People nowadays have too many options, and people have a hedonistic **mindset**. They think they deserve a little gourmet treat to enjoy once in a while and that leads to unhealthy eating habits and cholesterol blocked blood **vessels**.

> 生活方式改變－不健康的飲食習慣

■ 人們現今有許多選擇，而人們有享樂的心態。他們認為他們值得一些難得的樂事，偶爾享用美食，而這些都導致不健康的飲食習慣和膽固醇堵塞血管。

mindset 心態
vessel 血管

■ When you have less food and **entertainment** options, everything becomes simple, and of course leads to a longer **lifespan**.

> 生活方式改變－較少的選擇時

■ 當你對於食物和娛樂有著較少的選擇時，每件事都變得簡單了，而理所當然的有著較長的壽命。

entertainment 娛樂
lifespan 壽命

消費習慣和偏好：大型百貨公司還是小型特色用品店

MP3 002

消費習慣和偏好－買符合需求的東西

■ After all it is your money that you spend, right? Plus, money is **hard to earn**. You have to choose something that is really **suitable** for your need.

■ 畢竟是用你的錢買的，對吧？再說，錢很難賺。你必須選擇一些對你來說真的符合需求的東西。

hard to earn 難賺
suitable 符合的

消費習慣和偏好－謹慎選擇才不後悔

■ I can't believe some people don't even look at the **manufacturing** dates and put all the groceries in the shopping cart, and only to regret later on that it has unhealthy **contents** in there.

■ 我不相信有些人不用看製造日期就能放整個貨品到購物車裡，然後於稍後後悔購買的東西有不健康成分在裡頭。

manufacturing 製造的
content 成分

消費習慣和偏好－喜歡眾多商品陳列的感覺

■ Definitely large grocery stores and department stores. I just want the feeling of an array of goods and **merchandise** when I walk into a store.

■ 當然是大型的食品雜貨店和百貨公司。我就是想要當我走進店裡時，數列貨物和商品陳列的感覺。

merchandise 商品

消費習慣和偏好－賞心悅目的感覺

■ So **pleasing to the eyes**. It's like the wow moment, and they have this and that... you can discuss those things with your friends, and the **excitement** of being in a large department store last like forever.

■ 也太賞心悅目。這就像是「哇」時刻，而且大型百貨公司有這個和那個... 你可以與你的朋友們討論那些商品，而且在大型百貨公司的興奮感像是永久持續般。

pleasing to the eyes 賞心悅目
excitement 興奮感

消費習慣和偏好－小型店太擁擠

■ I can't **tolerate** any of my friends who drag me to small specialty stores for shopping. I guess one person being in the store would be too **crowded**... .

■ 我不能忍受我的朋友拉我到小型特色用品店購物。我想一個人置身其中都嫌太擠吧!...。

tolerate 忍受
crowded 擁擠的

■ Have you heard from what **psychologists** say that too many options make it harder for people to **choose** what to buy, and I have to agree with them on this one.

消費習慣和偏好－太多選擇

■ 你有聽過心理學家稱的太多選擇會使人更難對於所要購買的東西做出選擇嗎？而且我必須在這個論述中同意心理學家們所說的。

psychologist 心理學家
choose 選擇

■ Being in large grocery stores and department stores might be **fancy** and include thousands of goods, but for some reason, you can't make a decision about which **brand** is much better.

消費習慣和偏好－較難做出選擇

■ 置身在大型的食品雜貨店和百貨公司可能感覺奢華和包含上千種商品，但是基於某些理由，你很難對於哪個品牌較好做出選擇。

fancy 奢華的
brand 品牌

居住問題：選擇待在大城市還是郊區

MP3 003

> 郊區－
> 監視器僅
> 是裝飾

- Setting an **alarm system** seems of little or no use. Most important of all, surveillance cameras are just decorations. When there is a robbery, policemen can't possibly gather any evidence because they usually find out that the **surveillance cameras** in the countryside are broken.

- 裝配警報系統幾乎沒有效果。最重要的是，監視器僅是裝飾品。當有搶劫發生時，警察們無法收集任何證據因為他們通常發現在郊區的監視器毀壞了。

alarm system 警報系統
surveillance camera 監視器

■ I do think living in a big city is much better. It's all about **safety**. Living in the big city makes you feel safe, and there are several **police stations** around.

大城市－
有警察局

■ 我認為居住在大城市較好。都是與安全性有關。居住在大城市使你感到安全，而且附近會有幾個警察局在。

safety 安全性
police station 警察局

■ You don't have to worry about there being a home **invasion**…I'm not being **paranoid**. It happens all the time. Home invasions often occur in the countryside.

大城市－
不用擔心
住宅入侵

■ 你不用擔心會有人入侵住宅…我不是患有妄想症。這總是發生。住宅入侵的事情通常在鄉村地區常發生。

invasion 入侵
paranoid 偏執的

大城市－
工作機會充足

■ Job opportunities **abound** in big cities. That's why there is always a gap between the number of people living in the city and the number of people living in the **suburban towns**.

■ 在大城市裡頭工作機會充足。這就是為什麼住在城市裡的人數和住在郊區小鎮裡的人數總是有差距。

abound 充足
suburban town 郊區小鎮

大城市－
便利性高

■ Living in the city is more convenient. You walk three blocks on the street, and there are an MRT station and U-bikes. The **commute time** for you from your home to the office is probably only twenty minutes.

■ 住在城市裡頭比較方便。你在街上走三個街區，然後那裡就有捷運站和 U-bike。從你家到辦公室的通勤時間可能只要花費 20 分鐘左右。

commute time 通勤時間

■ Definitely the countryside. I'm not having a second thought about this question. I just don't want to have another **purification** of the **lung** thing again.

鄉下地區－
健康因素 ❶

■ 當然是居住在鄉下地區。對於這個問題我絲毫沒有任何猶豫。當然鄉村地區囉。我不想要再次地清潔一次我的肺。

purification 淨化
lung 肺

■ Imagine how many wastes I **unconsciously** breath into the lung, and most of them are **lingered** into the lung.

鄉下地區－
健康因素 ❷

■ 想像一下有多少的廢棄物，我無意識下吸進肺部，而且大多數廢棄物質留在肺裡頭。

unconsciously 無意識地
linger 殘留

交通 ❶：工作、生活或旅遊中所偏好的交通工具

🎧 MP3 004

交通－
腳踏車 ❶

■ The **enjoyment** of taking a bicycle is beyond anything. Exercising **pacifies** your mind and burns extra calories. In addition, exercising eases your stress and it is especially helpful when you take a bike to work.

■ 搭乘腳踏車的享受超過任何事情。運動緩和心智而且燃燒額外的卡路里。此外，運動舒緩你的壓力而且對於騎乘腳踏車上班的人來說特別有幫助。

enjoyment 享受
pacify 緩和

交通－
腳踏車 ❷

■ Even though you have to like **go an extraordinary length** to take an **extra** suit to work and change it, you can totally feel like Sandra Bullock in *The Proposal*.

■ 即使你必須要大費周張攜帶額外的套裝到工作場合並做更換，你可以全然感到像是在「愛情限時簽」電影中珊卓・布拉克那樣。

go an extraordinary length 大費周張
extra 額外的

■ Taking a train makes you relaxed during the journey of the trip, and you get to see all the beautiful **scenery passing by in swift review**.

交通－
火車 ❶

■ 旅程途中期間搭火車讓你感到放鬆，而且美麗的景色很快速地映入眼簾。

scenery 景色
passing by in swift review
很快速地映入眼簾

■ Things have always been **hectic** with work and love life and so on... sitting on the train, you eventually have a little time to **reflect** on things happening lately.

■ 總是因為工作和感情生活等等的事感到忙亂…坐在火車內,你最終有點時間去思考最近所發生的事情

hectic 忙亂的
reflect 思考

■ You can feel the **breeze** coming from all the **bystanders** when you are driving. The polished windshield and the car totally represent the kind of the person a car driver himself.

■ 當你開車時,你可以感覺到一股微風從旁觀者那頭吹過來。光鮮亮麗的擋風玻璃和車子全然可以代表著汽車駕駛本身。

breeze 微風
bystander 旁觀者

交通一
汽車 ❷

- I'm not going to brag about the car I'm driving, but I do **enjoy** being **the center of the attention**.

- 我不是要吹牛自己所駕駛的車子，但是我會喜愛成為關注的焦點。

enjoy 喜愛
the center of the attention 關注的焦點

交通一
汽車 ❸

- In addition, seeing other **colleagues** driving motorcycles to work during the rainy day is just so **painful to watch**. They might catch a cold even with the raincoat on.

- 此外，看到其他同事們在雨天時騎乘摩托車，很慘不忍睹。他們即使穿著雨衣也可能會感冒。

colleague 同事
painful to watch 慘不忍睹

1
生活、娛樂、科技和交通

2
異國飲食和人文風情

3
教育、知識、學習

4
工作和金錢的使用

Unit 05 科技對生活造成的改變：閱讀紙張印刷品還是選擇電子書

MP3 005

■ With e-books, you can read them anywhere... as long as you carry your **smartphone** or other digital device. You can read it on the train without having a book **weighing down your legs** or hands.

電子書－火車上閱讀 ❶

■ 有了電子書，你可以到哪都能閱讀…只要你攜帶著你的智慧型手機或其他數位裝置。你在火車上閱讀而不用有著一本書壓著你的雙腳或者手需要支撐書。

smartphone 智慧型手機
weighing down your legs
壓著你的雙腳

電子書－
火車上閱讀
❷

■ You click close, and there you go, you get off the train. You can even **bookmark** the page you just finished. It's just a major **transformation** that people need to get used to it.

■ 你點下關閉，然後你就可以結束閱讀、下火車。你甚至可以標籤你剛看完的頁面。這就是主要的改變，而人們就是需要適應它。

bookmark 標籤
transformation 轉變

電子書－
對眼睛的傷害

■ Plus, reading information through the screen causes **eyestrain**. The blue light harms one's eyes and that's why a lot of people cannot look at the computer screen and smartphone screen for longer hours.

■ 再說，透過螢幕觀看訊息會導致眼睛疲勞。藍光會傷害眼睛而且這就是為什麼許多人無法於電腦螢幕和智慧型手機螢幕上觀看較長的一段時間。

eyestrain 眼睛疲勞

書籍－
沒有看螢幕
傷眼的困擾

■ With books and **newspapers**, you won't have that kind of problems. You are free to read **as long as you want**.

■ 如果是書籍和報紙的話，你就不會有那樣子的問題。你可以想要閱讀多久就閱讀多久。

newspaper 報紙
as long as you want 想要多久都可以

電子書－
是趨勢

■ I don't understand why people so **fixating** on books can't just **think outside of the box**. It's the trend.

■ 我不能理解為什麼執著於書的人，就是不能跳脫框架思考呢？ 這是趨勢。

fixate 執著於
think outside of the box 跳脫框架

電子書－
藍光眼鏡減低
影響

- Even if reading things through digital devices can cause eyestrain, there are eyeglasses that can significantly **reduce** the **effects** blue light has on our eyes, ok?

- 即使透過數位裝置閱讀會造成眼睛疲勞，有眼鏡能降低藍光對我們眼睛的影響，是吧？

reduce 降低
effect 效果

電子書－
食物和維他命
能護眼

- There are foods and **vitamins** that can protect you from those **problems**.

- 食物和維他命能保護你免於那些問題。

vitamin 維他命
problem 問題

MP3 006

■ My favorite season is Autumn because it is the best season to enjoy **crabs**. My favorite thing to do is to go to a seafood **restaurant** with my family and order seasonal made-to-order stream crabs.

最喜歡的
季節－秋天
肥美的秋蟹

■ 我最喜歡的季節是秋天，因為秋天的螃蟹最肥美！我最喜歡做的事就是跟我家人到海鮮餐廳去點季節限定現點現做的清蒸秋蟹。

crab 螃蟹
restaurant 餐廳

- I love Winter, and I love going to the hot spring. Hot springs are very good for your health. The proper way to do it is to **soak** in the hot spring first then jump into the cold one for a **brief** moment.

- 我最愛冬天了，而且我喜歡冬天去泡溫泉。其實泡溫泉對身體很好，泡溫泉正確的方式是先泡溫泉，然後簡短地泡一下冷泉。

soak 浸泡
brief 短暫的

最喜歡的
季節－冬天
泡溫泉

- I always **volunteer** to do the beach watch in Summer because I get to look cool in my board shorts and **show off my muscles**!

- 我夏天常常自願到海邊去當救生員，因為我可以正大光明的穿著我的海灘褲秀肌肉！

volunteer 自願
show off my muscles 秀肌肉

最喜歡的季
節－夏天穿著
海灘褲秀肌肉

1 生活、娛樂、科技和交通

2 異國飲食和人文風情

3 教育、知識、學習

4 工作和金錢的使用

最喜歡的
季節－夏天
曬古銅色肌膚

■ I love Summer; I think my **skin tone** says it all! I love spending time **under the sun** to build a nice tan. Trust me, the ladies love it!

■ 我最愛夏天，看我的膚色也知道。我喜歡在戶外曬太陽，曬成古銅色。相信我，女生都很吃這套！

skin tone 膚色
under the sun 在太陽下

戶外地點
－墾丁海灘
層層的椰子樹

■ There are lots of beaches in Kenting, but my favourite spot is the beach called Bai-sha which means white **sandy** beach in Chinese. It is a **secluded** area hidden among the palm trees.

■ 墾丁有很多海灘，可是我有個最愛的景點叫白砂，白砂中文的意思就是白色的沙灘。那是一個隱密的地方，被層層的椰子樹圍住。

sandy 覆蓋著沙的
secluded 隱密的

■ I love the hot springs in Bei-Tou, and my favourite **outdoor** hot spring is in this boutique hotel. Their hot spring area literately **hangs off** the cliff, and you feel like you are surrounded by mountains when you are in it.

戶外地點－
北投溫泉群山
環繞的感覺

■ 我喜歡北投的溫泉，而且我發現了一個泡溫泉最棒的地點，就是這間精品飯店。它的溫泉區就是真的是懸掛在山邊，在那裡你真的可以感受到群山環繞的感覺。

outdoor 戶外的
hang off 懸掛

■ My favourite outdoor place would have been the **roof top** of my building. It is like my **secret hide** out as well.

戶外地點－
家裡頂樓
獨處的好地方

■ 我最喜歡的戶外景點就是我家的頂樓了！那也是我的私房景點，獨處的地方。

roof top 屋頂
secret hide 祕密的藏匿處

041

MP3 007

- Where shall I start with my **smartphone**? Smartphone is everything in one! It is a phone, a camera, a **calculator**, a computer and so much more!

智慧型手機
❶

- 我該從何說起呢？智慧型手機簡直是集所有優點於一身，它是手機，也是相機，計算機還是台電腦呢！還有其他數不清的功能。

smartphone 智慧型手機
calculator 計算機

智慧型手機 ❷

■ I was not a smartphone user until pretty late. I was a bit **resentful** about learning new **technology**.

■ 我不是一開始就是個智慧型手機的支持者，剛開始我也很排斥新科技。

resentful 恨的
technology 科技

智慧型手機 ❸

■ Before I got my first smartphone, I didn't **understand** why people get **addicted to** their phone, but now I can't live without my phone.

■ 在我拿到第一支智慧型手機之前，我不懂為什麼有人會對手機上癮，可是我現在真的不能沒有我的手機。

understand 了解
be addicted to 上癮

智慧型手機
④

- I have to **check** my emails when I am out and about for work. I had to bring my **laptop** with me everywhere I went before, but all I need now is my smartphone.

- 我在外面出差時需要不斷地察看電子郵件。以前我到哪裡都一定要帶我的筆記型電腦，現在我只需要我的手機。

check 檢查
laptop 筆記型電腦

智慧型手機
⑤

- If I want to **scan** some information to share with my coworker, all I have to do is take a photo with my smartphone, then send it as an **attachment** to my email. This is definitely revolutionary !

- 就算我需要掃描文件給我的同事看，我也只要拿手機照張相，然後用郵件附件傳出去。這真是太劃時代了！

scan 掃描
attachment 附件

智慧型手機
❻

■ My favorite **function** is skype. I can **check on** my boyfriend all the time.

■ 我最喜歡的功能其實是 Skype 視訊，我隨時隨地都可以查我男朋友在哪裡。

function 功能
check on 查視

智慧型手機
❼

■ If I was**n't sure** whether he is **telling** me **the truth**, I will get him to put skype on, so I can see where he is.

■ 如果我覺得他沒有講實話，我就叫他開視訊，讓我看看他在哪裡。

not sure 不確定
tell the truth 說實話

MP3 008

■ I like to have a good laugh, so **comedy** is always my go to. My favorite is the "Hangover". It is about a group of friends deciding to go to Vegas to **celebrate** the bucks' night.

喜劇電影－
醉後大丈夫
❶

■ 我覺得人生就是要開心，所以看電影我也喜歡看喜劇。我最喜歡的騙子就是「醉後大丈夫」。這部片子是在講有關一群朋友決定到拉斯維加斯去慶祝單身的最後一夜。

comedy 喜劇
celebrate 慶祝

喜劇電影－
醉後大丈夫
❷

■ They accidently got drugged, so they had no **recollection** of what actually happened the night before. All they know is the groom is missing, and they have to find him in time for the wedding.

■ 但是他們卻意外地被下藥，完全不記得前晚發生過什麼事。他們只知道新郎不見了，一定要把他在婚禮前及時找回來。

recollection 回憶

電影－
浪漫愛情片

■ I love the girly movies, a sweet love story would be ideal. I also prefer **a happy ending** because most of the love stories in real life do not have **fairytale endings**.

■ 我喜歡浪漫愛情片，最好就是很甜蜜的故事。我也喜歡皆大歡喜的結局，因為現實生活中很難真的有童話故事般的愛情。

a happy ending 皆大歡喜的結局
fairytale endings 童話故事般的結局

1
生活、娛樂、科技和交通

2
異國飲食和人文風情

3
教育、知識、學習

4
工作和金錢的使用

■ I am a big fan of **special effects** and science fiction; I cannot **resist** the Si-Fi movies, such as "Starwars" and "Avatar." I think watching movies is a way to escape from reality.

■ 我超愛看有特效的故事，像星際大戰或是阿凡達那種科幻片我一定會去看。我覺得看電影就是要有想像空間。

電影－
特效電影

special effects 特效
resist 抗拒

■ Love songs are not my cup of tea. I find most of the love songs are just **corny** and **predictable**. Either you like that girl but the girl doesn't love you back, or you are happily in love with someone.

■ 情歌真的不是我的菜。我覺得大部分的情歌都很老套又一成不變，不是你愛那個女孩而那個女孩不愛你，就是目前戀愛 ING。

歌曲－
覺得情歌老套

corny 老套的
predictable 可預測的

1 生活、娛樂、科技和交通

歌曲－
喜歡聽情歌

■ I love the love songs because I always imagine I will meet my **Mr. Right** one day and live happily ever after just like what the **lyrics** say.

■ 我很喜歡聽情歌，因為我總是幻想著有一天我會遇到我的真命天子，過得幸福美滿，就像歌詞裡寫的一樣。

Mr. Right 真命天子
lyrics 歌詞

2 異國飲食和人文風情

3 教育、知識、學習

歌曲－
覺得情歌
有共鳴

■ I **don't mind** love songs because some of them really touch me heart especially when my **ex-girlfriend** decided to walk out on me a couple of years ago.

■ 我不介意聽情歌，因為有些歌我覺得寫得很好，很有共鳴。尤其是幾年前我剛跟我前女友分手的時候。

don't mind 不介意
ex-girlfriend 前女友

4 工作和金錢的使用

MP3 009

■ I've been to several National Parks in the world, but I would tell you that Jiuzhaigou Vally National Park in China is just magical.The **five-colored** lakes, the clear sky and the **evergreen** forests are just amazing on its own.

中國的九寨溝國家公園

■ 我有去過全世界很多座國家公園，但是我覺得最夢幻的是中國的九寨溝國家公園。五色沼、晴朗的天空和常青的森林分開看就已經很美了。

five-colored 五色的
evergreen 常綠的

■ I've been to Arenal National Park in Costa Rica. I heard many movies were shot in that National park. It's just so **lush** and there is an **active** volcano within the national park!

哥斯大黎加的 Arenal 國家公園

■ 我有去過哥斯大黎加的 Arenal 國家公園。我聽説很多電影在那裡拍攝過。那裡真的很翠綠，而且還有一個活火山在國家公園裡。

lush 蒼翠繁茂的
active 活躍的（此指火山）

■ Yes, I've been to Yosemite National Park. The **view** there is just **breathtaking**. I went in spring and that was when all the wildflowers were in bloom.

優勝美地國家公園 ❶

■ 有啊，我有去過優勝美地國家公園。那裡的景色真的美不勝收。我是春天的時候去的，在那個時候所有的野花都盛開。

view 景色
breathtaking 令人屏息的

■ Besides, the **crystalline** lakes and the pine forests just make perfect **postcard**-worthy views all around you!

■ 除此之外，清澈的湖水和松樹森林讓你周遭的景色都好像明信片一樣。

crystalline 水晶般的
postcard 明信片

國家公園與野生動物

■ I expect to see a lot of wildlife in the National Parks for sure. Some National Parks even give out maps of where to see those animals. Bear, **bighorn sheep**, **bison**, elk, and river otters all wander in the parks.

■ 我一定是預期在國家公園裡看到很多野生動物。有一些國家公園甚至會給你一個地圖去看動物。熊、大角羊、美洲野牛、麋鹿和水獺都在公園裡到處遊蕩。

bighorn sheep 大角羊
bison 美洲野牛

國家公園與熊

■ I was once really close to a bear. It was **frightening**, but also amazing to see a bear in such a short distance. I was in awe to see such a beautiful **creature** in the National Parks.

■ 我有一次很接近一隻熊。其實蠻恐怖的，但是同時也是很神奇可以這麼近看著熊。我那時候看到這麼美的生物真的很震撼。

frightening 使人驚嚇的
creature 生物

國家公園與實際感受

■ I've always imagined the stars are all over the place in the National Parks, the forests and all that jazz.

■ 我總是想像在國家公園裡到處都是星星、森林諸如此類的。

imagine 想像
star 星星

1 生活、娛樂、科技和交通

2 異國飲食和人文風情

3 教育、知識、學習

4 工作和金錢的使用

運動：女子世界盃足球
賽、NBA 季後賽、紐約
市空中瑜珈

MP3 010

女子世界
盃足球賽

■ I was **invited** to the 2015 FIFA Women's World Cup in **Canada** because a friend I grew up with was playing for USA.

■ 我有一個從小長大的朋友他代表美國隊參賽，所以我受邀去加拿大看 2015 年的女子世界盃足球賽。

invite 邀請
Canada 加拿大

■ I got the VIP seats to watch the game and joined them for the after party to celebrate the victory. It was quite an experience to **witness** my friend add World Cup Champion to her already amazing career.

VIP 座位

■ 我有 VIP 座位，而且後來還加入她們慶祝勝利的派對。親眼看到我朋友把世足冠軍列入她本來就很好的職業生涯真的是很棒的經驗。

witness 目睹

■ I went on **a road trip** in California. It was during the time of the NBA **playoffs**, we couldn't pass the game in Los Angeles when the Lakers are playing against the Miami Heat.

NBA 季後賽

■ 我到加州公路旅行，那個時候正好是 NBA 季後賽的時候，所以我們不想錯過在加州的湖人隊跟邁阿密熱火隊的賽事。

a road trip 公路旅行
playoffs 季後賽

1 生活、娛樂、科技和交通

2 異國飲食和人文風情

3 教育、知識、學習

4 工作和金錢的使用

■ It was quite an **exciting** game to watch. You can't beat live NBA playoffs. It was totally **worth** the drive.

現場的 NBA 季後賽

■ 那場比賽真的很刺激，而且你真的無法超越現場的 NBA 季後賽。完全值得我們開那麼遠的車去看。

exciting 令人感到興奮的
worth 值得

■ I tried the **Aerial** Yoga in New York City when I was on a business trip last time. It definitely **turned my world upside down**.

紐約市空中瑜珈

■ 我上次去紐約市出差的時候有試過空中瑜珈。那真的是把我的世界弄得翻天覆地的。

aerial 空中的
turned my world upside down 把我的世界弄得翻天覆地的

吊床來
練習瑜珈和
皮拉提斯

■ It's basically the combination of Yoga and **Pilates** with the use of a **hammock**. I felt really good after the workout.

■ 那其實就是用吊床來練習瑜珈和皮拉提斯的綜合版。我在運動後真的覺得很棒。

Pilates 皮拉提斯
hammock 吊床

莫斯科有嘗試
尾流衝浪

■ I tried wake surfing in **Moscow**. It's really cool because you are basically surfing the wake created by the **boat** in front of you.

■ 我在莫斯科有嘗試尾流衝浪。那很酷因為你就是在衝你前面的船幫你製造出來的浪。

Moscow 莫斯科
Boat 船

音樂：爵士樂、雷鬼樂、獨立搖滾和紐奧良的典藏廳

MP3 011

■ There are so many **emotions** in Jazz and I always feel like when people are talking about music being **contagious**, I think they are referring to Jazz.

爵士樂
具感染力

■ 爵士樂裡有很多的情緒。當大家在說音樂很有感染力的時候，我都想說他們一定是在說爵士樂。

emotion 情緒
contagious 有感染力的

■ I'm gonna go with Reggae. I've been traveling in a lot of islands, and they start to **grow on me** one day, and before I know it, I'm **humming** the reggae tunes all day.

雷鬼樂

■ 我應該是會選雷鬼樂。我已經在很多的島嶼旅行過了。突然有一天我漸漸開始喜歡雷鬼樂，然後在我反應過來之前，我已經整天都在哼雷鬼的調子了。

grow on me 漸漸開始喜歡
hum 哼

■ I think all my favorite songs **belong to** Indie Rock, so I **assume** that's my favorite type of music.

獨立搖滾 ❶

■ 我覺得好像我很喜歡的歌都是獨立搖滾，所以我想那應該是我最喜歡的音樂種類吧！

belong to 屬於
assume 假定

1 生活、娛樂、科技和交通

2 異國飲食和人文風情

3 教育、知識、學習

4 工作和金錢的使用

■ The best one was at the Preservation Hall in New Orleans. It's like the holy ground for all jazz **fans**. I had my **doubts** before it started because it was in a tiny and old building with no seats or air-conditioning.

紐奧良的
典藏廳

■ 我聽過最棒的是在紐奧良的典藏廳。那裡就像是爵士樂迷們的聖地一樣。我在表演開始之前有我的疑慮因為那棟建築又小又舊而且又沒有座位和冷氣。

doubt 疑慮
fan 迷

■ I was backpacking in **New Zealand** when my Couch Surfing host took me to this family fair. It was really fun with a lot of rides and food **stands**.

紐西蘭
當背包客

■ 我在紐西蘭當背包客的時候,我沙發衝浪的主人帶我去一個家庭園遊會。那裡真的很好玩,而且也有很多遊樂設施和小吃攤。

New Zealand 紐西蘭
stand 攤

西班牙公園的
地下道 ❶

■ I was walking at the **underground** of a park in Spain and that was when I came across this amazing street artist. He's a guitarist, and really all he did was just playing **guitar** there.

■ 我在西班牙一個公園的地下道走路時，突然遇到這個超厲害的街頭藝人。他是一個吉他手，然後他真的也只是在彈吉他而已。

underground 地下道
guitar 吉他

西班牙公園的
地下道 ❷

■ But the **sound** was very crisp with the **echoes** from the underground, it became very powerful music. There were people stopping here, and I stayed the whole time.

■ 但是吉他的聲音很清脆，而且因為在地下道有回音就讓整個音樂十分的強烈。人們也因為音樂表演停在那，而表演期間我都待在那裡。

sound 聲音
echo 回音

MP3 012

■ They are all unique in their own ways. Who doesn't like Disney Land really? Cinderella's **castle**, the **carousel**, and all the magic in the park. It feels like a dream come true when I'm in Disney Land.

迪士尼樂園

■ 不過說真的怎麼可能會有人不喜歡迪士尼樂園？仙杜瑞拉的城堡、旋轉木馬還有園內所有的魔法。在迪士尼樂園裡就好像是夢想成真一樣！

castle 城堡
carousel 旋轉木馬

Schlitterbahn
的水上樂園 ❶

■ My favorite amusement park is actually a water park called Schlitterbahn. It hands down the best amusement park in the world. The countless water slides are all very long and fun.

■ 我最喜歡的遊樂園其實是一間叫做 Schlitterbahn 的水上樂園。它真的是我認為世界上最棒的遊樂園。數不清的滑水道都很長又很好玩。

Schlitterbahn
的水上樂園 ❷

■ You can carry the tubes around the park to do all kinds of slides or just float around the **floating** river. There are always long lines, but no one seems to care too much once they get on the ride.

■ 你在園內也都可以拿著游泳圈去各式各樣的滑水道，或是只是在漂漂河上漂。雖然都要排隊很久，但是大家都是坐到之後就不會在意了。

tube 滑水道

1
生活、娛樂、科技和交通

2
異國飲食和人文風情

3
教育、知識、學習

4
工作和金錢的使用

■ The Universal's Islands of adventures in Orlando! It's both **intriguing** and exciting. Once you graduate from Disney Land, you would enjoy this place so much.

■ 在奧蘭多的環球影城冒險島樂園！它又好玩又刺激。你在迪士尼樂園畢業之後，你就會很喜歡這個地方。

intriguing 引起興趣的

■ It was a walking tour through the whole haunted house. Everything in the haunted house was as if they came out directly from the **crime scene**. I had nightmares and was scared to go to any haunted house after that one.

■ 那是一個要走路穿過鬼屋的行程。每一個在那個鬼屋裡面的東西都好像是直接從犯罪現場搬來的。我再去玩那個鬼屋之後就做惡夢，而且還從此對鬼屋有陰影。

crime scene 犯罪現場

卡在摩天輪上

■ I didn't mind it, but it gets scary because we didn't know when we could get back to the ground. It was pretty windy up there, too. Then, I started to have flashbacks about those **horrifying scenes** from the scary movies.

■ 我一開始是不介意，但是後來越來越可怕因為我們不知道什麼時候才可以回到陸地上。而且在上面的時候風也很大。然後我腦海就開始有一些恐怖片裡面的恐怖情節畫面。

horrifying scenes 恐怖的情景

雲霄飛車

■ I got motion sickness when I was on a roller coaster ride. My best friend at the time was nice enough to sit me down at the chair nearby and listened to how **dizzy** I felt the whole time.

■ 我坐完雲霄飛車的時候開始有點暈。我那時候最好的朋友人很好的帶我去坐在附近的椅子上，而且還全程一直聽我說我有多暈。

dizzy 暈眩的

MP3 013

■ The best one I've been to is La Louvre in Paris. The museum itself is an art already, not to mention the **famous artworks** inside. It took me a while to wait till it was my turn to see Mona Lisa.

巴黎的羅浮宮

■ 我去過最棒的博物館是在巴黎的羅浮宮。博物館本身就是一個藝術品了，更別提在裡面那些有名的藝術品。我那時候等了蠻久才換我看蒙娜麗莎的微笑。

famous 著名的
artwork 藝術品

夏威夷
歐胡島的主教
博物館 ❶

■ However, Bishop Museum in Oahu, Hawaii is a really fun museum. It demonstrates how **lava** is formed and there are a lot of activities and performances at certain time of the day, such as Hula Dance performance.

■ 但是在夏威夷歐胡島的主教博物館是一個很好玩的博物館。它展示了岩漿是怎麼形成的，而且那裡不一樣的時間也都有不一樣的表演，例如草裙舞表演。

lava 火山岩

義大利烏非茲
博物館 ❶

■ I thought Uffizi Gallery was an **excellent** museum. It was overwhelming to see all the famous works gathered together in one museum.

■ 我覺得義大利烏非茲博物館是博物館裡面的翹楚。在一個博物館裡面看到那麼多有名的作品其實蠻震撼的。

excellent 卓越的

義大利烏非茲
博物館 ❷

■ Michelangelo, Da Vinci, Raphael and more. I took my time walking from room to room and trying to **absorb** the fact that those were the works that I read from history books in class.

■ 米開朗基羅、達文西、拉斐爾等等。我在每個展示間裡都慢慢地逛然後盡可能地相信在我眼前都是在歷史課本裡面讀到的那些作品。

absorb 吸收

美國薩莫維爾
市的糟糕藝術
博物館 ❶

■ I heard there's a Museum of Bad Art at Somerville Mass. That's just so out of the box! **Normally**, we see amazing or beautiful arts in a museum.

■ 我有聽説一間在美國薩莫維爾市的糟糕藝術博物館。那真是太有創意了。通常我們都只會在博物館裡看見很棒或是很美的藝術。

normally 通常

克羅埃西亞的
失戀博物館
❶

■ The Museum of Broken Relationships in **Croatia** is by far the strangest museum I've heard. What do you do with the stuff that belongs to your past **relationships**?

■ 在克羅埃西亞有一間失戀博物館是我目前為止聽過最奇怪的博物館。你失戀之後都怎麼處理那些屬於之前戀情的東西啊？

Croatia 克羅埃西亞
relationship 戀情

克羅埃西亞的
失戀博物館
❷

■ I put them in a box or throw them away, but this museum is looking for those **remnants** of a **broken** relationship. It's really strange but I'm with them.

■ 我都把它們放到箱子裡或是丟掉，可是這間博物館都在找那些過去戀情遺留下的的東西。那真的很奇怪，但是我蠻喜歡他們的點子的。好有創意。

remnant 遺留物
broken 損壞的

交通 ❷：Uber、威尼斯私人導覽、越南坐嘟嘟車和佛羅里達州電動代步車

MP3 014

選擇司機兼導遊的服務

■ I **usually go with** the driver guide service. I really don't feel like handling the stress of looking for **directions** or getting lost when I'm traveling. I just want to use the time in the most efficient way.

■ 我通常會選擇司機兼導遊的服務。我真的很不想要在旅行的時候還要煩惱找路，或是迷路。我只是想要有效率地利用時間。

usually go with 通常會選擇
direction 方向

搭便車

■ I usually hitch hike when I'm traveling. You will be **amazed** at how many kind people there are in the world. Sometimes it only takes me 5 minutes to get a ride, but sometimes it takes **a couple of hours**.

■ 我在旅行的時候通常喜歡搭便車。你會很驚訝世界上有多少好人。有的時候只會花五分鐘，可是有的時候要等好幾個小時。

amaze 驚訝
a couple of hours 幾小時

Uber

■ It's a new thing though, it's pretty much an app you can **request** rides from where you are. It's usually **cheaper** than a taxi, so there you go!

■ 不過那個還蠻新的。其實它就是一個 APP 你可以在你所在的地方叫車。而且通常他還比計程車便宜，當然是選他囉！

request 要求
cheaper 更便宜

■ I was in Venice and of course I had to try the Gondola ride, but I went with the **slightly** fancier one. My gondola offered a **private** tour and it came with the singers and the musicians.

威尼斯
私人導覽 ❶

■ 我在威尼斯的時候當然要試試看貢多拉，但是我是選了比一般高級一點點的。我的貢多拉有私人導覽，而且船上還有歌手和樂手。

slightly 稍微
private 私人的

■ It was really **romantic**, but I didn't really have a date, so it was actually a little bit **awkward**. Well, it was really cool though.

威尼斯
私人導覽 ❷

■ 真的很浪漫但是我那個時候沒有伴啦，所以其實有點尷尬。不過還是蠻酷的就是了。

romantic 浪漫的
awkward 笨拙的

越南坐嘟嘟車

- **Strange enough**, I enjoyed my ride as my driver was weaving through the traffic in the middle of Ho Chi Minh City. It was a pretty **unique** experience.

- 很奇怪的是，我的司機在胡志明市中穿梭在車陣之間時，我其實是還蠻喜歡的。那是一個蠻獨特的體驗。

strange enough 奇怪的是
unique 獨特的

**佛羅里達州
電動代步車**

- I was in Florida riding the Segway while I was touring around. I felt like a really **lazy** person from the future, but it was really **awesome**.

- 我在佛羅里達州的時候有用賽格威（電動代步車）到處遊覽。我那時候覺得我真的很像是從未來來的很懶惰的人，但是那真的很棒耶！

lazy 懶惰的
awesome 棒的

動物園和遊樂園體驗：
廚藝競賽、鱷魚脫逃、
親吻亭

MP3 015

動物園－遞棉
花糖給浣熊

■ You are able to take photos with animals, such as koalas and pandas. Have actual contact with them, such as handling **cotton** candy to **raccoons**, while filming how they end up ruining it.

■ 你能與像是無尾熊和貓熊這樣的動物拍照。實際與他們接觸，例如遞棉花糖給浣熊，邊攝影他們如何毀了棉花糖。

cotton 棉花
raccoon 浣熊

動物園－廚藝競賽

■ You also get to prepare food for them in the Zoo kitchen. In the afternoon, we're having a contest of prepared foods by attendees. Of course, animals will be the judge to decide which is more delicious.

■ 你可以在動物園廚房準備食物給牠們。在下午，我們會有替參加者準備好的食材做為競賽，當然動物們會是裁判評定哪道料理比較美味。

動物園－鱷魚事件❶

■ Our **crocodiles** are not in their **compartments**. But it's chilly out there. I'm not sure why they have to take a weekend getaway or something. I don't want you guys to panic.

■ 我們園內的鱷魚不在隔間裡。但是外頭相當寒冷。我不知道為什麼他們想要上演個周末大逃亡或什麼的。我不想要你們感到驚嚇。

crocodile 鱷魚
compartment 隔間

■ I've four animal **specialists** and police officers out there looking for them already. When you see them, just keep **calm**... and you'll be fine... OMG what are they doing out there.

■ 我已經派四個動物專人和警察們找尋他們。當你們看到他們就保持冷靜...我想你們會沒事的...天啊他們在這幹嘛...。

specialist 專家
calm 冷靜

■ Oops... My office glass wall just **shattered**. Apparently, I was fooled by Glass Company. It can't stand crocodile's **punch**.

■ 糟了...我的辦公司玻璃牆剛碎掉了。顯然我被玻璃公司騙了。它無法承受鱷魚的撞擊。

shatter 破碎
punch 撞擊

■ See the kissing **booth** over there… Too bad, I'm a **reporter**, or I will jump at the chance… they all look very gorgeous…

慈善親吻亭❶

■ 看那裡有個親吻亭…真不巧我是記者，否則我會抓住這好機會…他們看起來都很美…。

booth 亭
reporter 記者

■ There's a guy kissing a girl of my **dreams**… I can't watch it… there's another girl… seems she is sending me **mixed** signals… come join us…even if it's a long line here…

慈善親吻亭❷

■ 有個男子親了我夢想中女孩…我無法再看下去了…又有另一個女孩…似乎他正向我遞送混雜的訊號…來加入我們吧…即使這裡隊排的很長…。

dream 夢想
mixed 混合的

MP3 016

- First, we're going to give you an update on some **exhilarating** news. The whale that was found on **shallow** water has been saved. At least, he won't be the meal for brown bears.

新聞－
鯨魚擱淺

- 首先我們將給你關於最令人感到興奮的新聞的更新。被發現在淺水水域擱淺的鯨魚已被救了。至少他不會成為棕熊的食物了。

exhilarating 令人感到興奮的
shallow 淺水的

新聞－颱風逼近

■ Good afternoon it's the afternoon news. I can feel Florida **heat** even if I'm not outside. Let's see if an **approaching** tornado is gonna affect our weekend.

■ 下午好這是下午新聞。我能感受到佛羅里達州的熱即使我不在外頭。讓我們看即將逼近的颱風是否影響我們周末

heat 熱
approach 即將接近

新聞－路徑預測

■ Let me show you... see the **tornado** doubles its size when it reaches here... and it's getting bigger... it's gonna be the biggest in history... we're **predicting** two different routes...

■ 讓我們向你展示...看這颱風當它抵達這裡時體型成了雙倍...它漸漸增大...將會成為史上最大...我們正預測兩個不同路徑...。

tornado 颱風
predict 預測

■ First, it's gonna hit the Bahamas and land at Daytona and the second **route** would be **directly** landing at palm beach… no…not palm beach but cocoa beach…I guess people at Miami will feel so relieved…

■ 第一個是他們會先侵襲巴哈馬然後於蝶同那登陸，而第二個路徑是它可能直接在棕櫚海灘..不…不是棕櫚海灘而是可可亞海灘登陸...我想在邁阿密的人會感到如釋重負。

route 路徑
directly 直接地

■ Morning it's morning news. First, the important news about tunnel A. There've been several **landsides** happening, so it's **officially** closed.

■ 早安，這是早間新聞。首先，最重要的新聞是關於隧道 A。持續有幾個山崩的狀況發生。所以隧道正式關閉了。

landside 山崩
officially 正式地

■ Car drivers are suggested to take **tunnel** B instead or take Road 555 through the super high way. This problem won't be fixed until the weather is more stable, which according to our **newsman** it's gonna last until next Friday.

新聞一
隧道山崩❷

■ 建議開車的駕駛透過高速公路行駛隧道 B 或公路 555 號。根據我們新聞播報人員，此問題在天氣較穩定前不會修復好，且情況會持續到下週五

tunnel 隧道
newsman 新聞播報人員

■ Due to heavy rain and fog, the airport will be **temporarily** shut down for a while. For more flight information please visit our website. Front page.

新聞一
隧道山崩❸

■ 由於大雨傾盆，機場會暫時關閉。更多航班資訊，請瀏覽我們的網站。首頁。

temporarily 暫時地

1 生活、娛樂、科技和交通

2 異國飲食和人文風情

3 教育、知識、學習

4 工作和金錢的使用

MP3 017

廚房教學直播

■ Don't worry that you don't have any experience. Grab your apron and prepare all the **ingredients**. Best kitchen will show you how. Before we start, I'd like to show you my personal **weapon**... don't be afraid... it's not a gun... it's a pot.

■ 別擔心你不具備任何經驗。拿起你的圍裙和準備所有成分。倍斯特廚房將向你展示如何製作。在我們開始之前，我想要向你展示我的個人武器⋯別害怕⋯這不是槍⋯這是鍋具。

ingredient 成分
weapon 武器

082

廚房教學直播 ❷

■ It looks like it's **new** doesn't it, but I'm gonna tell you she is two years old... actually...it's been used for 23 months...that's almost two years... see just **a few scratches** here.

■ 這看起來想是新的，對不對?但是我要告訴你她兩年了⋯實際上她已經使用了 23 個月⋯算成兩年⋯看這裡只有幾個刮痕⋯。

new 新的
a few scratches 幾個刮痕

廚房教學直播 ❸

■ ... and really perfect for cooking fish and meat. I do have a really good oven **ideal** for cooking Thanksgiving turkey... let me **demonstrate** it for you.

■ 拿來煮魚和肉品真的很完美。我有很好的烤箱拿來煮感恩節的火雞是很理想的廚具⋯讓我向你展示。

ideal 理想的
demonstrate 展示

■ Best cinema will be having a **renovation** from June 20 to July 28. We're really sorry for the **inconvenience** caused. Good news is that we are adding several facilities.

■ 倍斯特電影將於 6 月 20 日到 7 月 28 日進行整修。我們對於引起的不便感到抱歉。好消息是我們將新增幾項設施。

renovation 裝修
inconvenience 不方便

■ It's gonna wow you when we **reopen**. I guess I'm gonna tell just a bit. For example, we are having a **ghost castle**.

■ 當我們重新開張時您會感到驚艷。我想我可以說一點點。例如，我們將有鬼屋城堡。

reopen 重新開張
ghost castle 鬼屋城堡

- Whoever makes it to the end of the castle will get a **free ticket**, but whoever quits or not being able to make it to the end will get **punished**.

電影院裝修 ❸

- 不論誰達到城堡終點都將獲得免費門票，但任何放棄或無法抵達終點的將會受到懲罰。

free ticket 免費門票
punish 懲罰

- Best Toy Company has earned its **reputation** not by providing the durable and eye-catching toys, but by providing **chemical-free** toys.

玩具公司－
安全玩具

- 倍斯特玩具公司不是以提供耐用和誘人的玩具聞名，而是以無化學物質的玩具聞名

reputation 名聲
chemical-free 不含化學物質的

大學是否該提供學生娛樂

MP3 018

■ Universities should not provide students with entertainment, such as movies or **concerts** on campus. It's an academic setting and can **digress** students a bit from studying.

提供學生娛樂－電影或音樂會

■ 大學不應該要提供學生娛樂，例如在校園內有電影或音樂會。這是學術環境，而且這會使學生學習分心。學生必定會被娛樂影響而分心。

concert 音樂會
digress 脫離

■ I just can't imagine a **situation** where professors allow students to use smartphones during the course and expect students to focus.

不該提供
學生娛樂－
學生難專注

■ 我就是無法想像一種情況，教授允許學生在上課期間使用智慧型手機，然後期待學生專注。

situation 情況

■ Imagine how much stress students are under studying all day, so it's ok to just loosen up a bit by watching a film right after a class... say International Law or Advanced Calculus. I just **don't see the harm** here.

提供學生
娛樂－
減壓放鬆

■ 想像學生在讀了一整天的書後有多少壓力，而且在課後看電影能放鬆一下，這是 ok 的…像是國際法律或高階微積分課後。我不認為有什麼壞處。

don't see the harm 不認為有什麼壞處

■ In addition, our **brain** needs the rest. With 8 hours of courses a day it's like the brain **has reached its limit**.

■ 此外，我們的大腦需要休息。每天八小時的課程對像是大腦來說已經達到的上限了。

brain 大腦
has reached its limit 已經達到極限

■ Watching films gives the brain exactly that and the film **eases** the **information** that students consume all day, so the brain restores itself.

■ 觀看電影確切地給予大腦它所需要的，而且電影舒緩了學生吸收一整天的資訊後的昏脹感，如此一來大腦會自我復原。

ease 舒緩
information 資訊

■ Haven't you heard all work and no play makes Jack a dull boy. It's just a two-hour movie…or an hour and 40 minutes... I don't know why some professors are **making a big deal about it**.

> 提供學生娛樂－教授小題大作

■ 你沒聽過只是工作而不遊戲會使人變得遲鈍。這只是兩小時的電影…或是一小時 40 分鐘…我不知道為什麼有些教授會為此小題大作。

making a big deal about it 為此小題大作

■ After you graduate who cares whether you got an A in History or an A+ in Economics. Employers and banks just don't care. It isn't like our future **rests** on academic success.

> 提供學生娛樂－學術表現和未來成就無關

■ 在你畢業後，誰在乎你在歷史課拿到 A 或是在經濟學拿到 A+ 呢？雇主和銀行就不在乎。別弄得好像是我們的未來都要仰賴學術成功。

rest 仰賴

Part2 介紹了世界各地的地點和美食，不需要真的親自走訪過這些地區，充分利用每個高分句和細節點，內化成自己的活潑表達句，讓考官感受到真實度和有親臨實境的感受。表達細節性程度越高代表越豐富，考試成績就更高喔！

Part

2

個人感受、經驗
和細節：異國飲
食和人文風情

MP3 019

■ Finally, I'm here – the historical city of the States, Boston. It **depressed** me to travel alone for business in this beautiful city at first. However, after I arrived, the fresh air and breeze welcomed me just like my **beloved** baby girl.

來到波士頓這美麗城市

■ 我總算到這兒來了，美國歷史悠久的都市—波士頓。本來要自己來這個美麗的城市出差還挺讓我沮喪的，不過，抵達之後的清新空氣和微風讓我覺得賓至如歸，就像我心愛的女孩在這兒歡迎我似的。

depress 沮喪
beloved 心愛的

■ Now I'm sitting here **sipping** on my creamy clam chowder, feeling the sunshine and the smell of sea water. My baby girl loves sea food. I remember our first date in a seafood restaurant.

> 品嚐蛤蠣巧達湯邊享受陽光和海洋的氣息

■ 現在,我邊坐在這兒品嚐蛤蠣巧達湯,邊享受陽光和海洋的氣息。我的女孩最喜歡海鮮,還記得第一次約會我們在一家海鮮餐館。

sipping 品嚐

■ She was impressed by the way I opened up a **lobster**. The chowder is full of flavor; I can almost taste the ocean down there in my bowl. The cream is like an embrace to my body.

> 湯滋味馥郁

■ 她對我獨到的開龍蝦方式大感驚奇。這道湯滋味馥郁,我甚至覺得在碗裡品嚐了整個海洋。奶油像擁抱般包裹我。

lobster 龍蝦

■ To truly enjoy a cup of drip **black coffee**, you must have someone to accompany you. There were mornings when I spent time in a **local** coffee shop.

■ 要真正享受一杯濾泡式黑咖啡，我必須有伴。有些早晨我會在當地的咖啡廳消磨時間。

black coffee 黑咖啡
local 當地的

享受一杯濾泡式黑咖啡

■ I'm no big fan of chocolate, but my husband definitely **has a sweet tooth**. He loves chocolate, especially a moist, **melt-in-the-mouth** chocolate chip muffin.

■ 我不是很喜歡巧克力，但外子頗嗜甜食。他愛死了巧克力，尤其是濕潤、入口即化的巧克力碎片瑪芬。

has a sweet tooth 嗜甜食
melt-in-the-mouth 入口即化的

巧克力碎片瑪芬蛋糕

蔓越莓嚐起來
酸澀微甜

■ Cranberries are **tangy** and a little bit sweet. It's like life, sometimes sweet but usually sour. Some people add a lot of sugar and make it into preserves. I don't. I like to taste the original flavor, knowing that the reality is harsh.

■ 蔓越莓嚐起來酸澀微甜，好像人生一般，常時苦澀，有時甜美。有人會加糖將蔓越莓作成果醬，我卻不好此道；我喜歡品嚐蔓越莓的原味，這讓我知道現實是嚴峻的。

tangy 酸的

麵包體本身
十分紮實

■ However, cranberry bread is a good way to eat cranberries. The bread itself is firm to touch, not too sweet but **filling**.

■ 不過呢，蔓越莓麵包倒是不錯的選擇。麵包體本身十分紮實，嘗來不過甜，且十分有飽足感，有一種踏實的感覺。

filling 踏實的

MP3 020

- The first time I tasted his **perfectly** mashed potatoes was on a normal day. I accidently stepped in a diner that I didn't plan to go to. What happened was **a row of coincidences**.

與完美的馬鈴薯泥相遇

- 我與完美的馬鈴薯泥相遇在一個普通的日子，那天我意外的踏入一間我沒想過要去的餐館用餐，接著發生的事是一連串的巧合。

perfectly 完美地
a row of coincidences 一連串的巧合

■ the chicken salad that I wanted was sold out, so I had a steak instead. And there it was – the little scoop of mashed potato sitting beside the steak, so clean and elegant. It was like the **fireworks** of the fourth of July in my head.

口感像是國慶煙火般在我腦海中綻放

■ 我想點的雞肉沙拉賣完了，所以我改點牛排。就是那客牛排一旁邊有一勺馬鈴薯泥，白淨又優雅的放在那兒。當我吃下一口馬鈴薯泥，它就像國慶煙火般在我腦海中綻放。

firework 煙火

■ It just **exploded** when I took it in my mouth. Then I totally ignored the steak and just stared at that mashed potato.

緊盯著那團馬鈴薯泥

■ 當我放進嘴裡時，就這樣炸開了。接著牛排便被我完全無視，我只能緊盯著那團馬鈴薯泥。很難察覺出這是誰做的。

explode 爆炸

1 生活、娛樂、科技和交通

2 異國飲食和人文風情

3 教育、知識、學習

4 工作和金錢的使用

■ It was a dream come true. The **smooth** mashed potato was like a **slide** that took me to simple happiness.

■ 這真是夢想成真。綿密軟糯的馬鈴薯泥是一道滑梯，帶我滑入純粹的幸福。

smooth 滑順的
slide 滑梯

■ After Laura recommends me to give it a try, I'm dying to know how a **bland carcass** in a shell can be so famous.

■ 蘿拉推薦我嘗嘗後，我也很想知道一個平淡無味的甲殼類到底是為什麼能這麼有名。

bland 平淡無味的
carcass 屍體

- It's actually an experience of **luxurious** delicate taste of meat, something a meat-and-potato **Texan** knows absolutely nothing about. So there it is, a whole boiled lobster in its shell on the dining table.

奢華的
肉品體驗

- 這是奢華細緻的肉品體驗，一個對德州佬全然陌生的東西。上菜了，一隻完整的水煮龍蝦被端上桌了。

luxurious 奢華的
Texan 德州佬

- Laura **carefully** shows me how to open the shells with the scissors and pliers. It requires patience and **prudence** to eat this meal.

用道具
劃開龍蝦殼

- 蘿拉小心翼翼地示範如何用剪刀和鉗子開龍蝦殼，吃這道菜還真需要耐心和細心哩。

carefully 小心翼翼地
prudence 細心

1 生活、娛樂、科技和交通

2 異國飲食和人文風情

3 教育、知識、學習

4 工作和金錢的使用

奶醬通心粉、熱烤鮪魚三明治

MP3 021

- So I still have two hours before dinner and I have **macaroni** and cheddar cheese here…what else do I need? Greens. Yes. We need to **go healthy**.

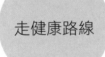
走健康路線

- 距離晚餐還有兩小時,通心粉和切達起司也準備好了。我還需要什麼?綠色蔬菜,對了,我們走健康路線。

macaroni 通心粉
go healthy 走健康路線

■ There is some frozen broccoli in the **freezer**. Perfect. What should I do with them though? Oh, I should thaw them in the **microwave**... okay.

拿到微波爐去解凍

■ 冷凍庫裡有花椰菜，完美。我該拿它們怎麼辦？喔，我要拿到微波爐去解凍…好。

freezer 冷凍庫
microwave 微波爐

■ So I'm gonna cook this macaroni and **mix** it with cheese sauce... right, that looks good. To the oven. Now, the broccoli is done too, it is hot and **steaming**.

煮通心粉

■ 現在我要煮通心粉，然後把它跟起司醬混合在一塊…好，看起來很棒，現在進烤箱。花椰菜也準備好了，還冒著熱煙呢。

mix 混合
steaming 冒煙的

■ Peep. You've got one **message**. It's her, Esther. I know what she wants even without reading the **SMS**: a tuna melt sandwich.

熱烤鮪魚起司三明治

■ 嗶。您有一則新訊息,是伊斯特。我不用看就知道她要什麼:一個熱烤鮪魚起司三明治。

message 訊息
SMS 手機簡訊

■ Esther enjoys the hot melting cheese on tuna so much, that just watching her eating gives me **pleasure**. I've tried to talk her into a steak or a **meatball** sandwich, but she always says "the old way is the best way".

熱烤鮪魚起司三明治的魔力

■ 伊斯特很喜歡熱烤鮪魚起司三明治,光看她吃就覺得幸福。我曾想說服她嘗試牛排三明治或肉丸三明治,但她總是說「老派最棒了」。

pleasure 樂趣
meatball 肉丸

多加鮪魚

- Today I'm giving her some **extra** tuna, hoping that inside of the simple goodness she can taste **a hint of my affection**.

- 今天我在三明治裡加了多一點點的鮪魚,希望她在簡單的美味中嘗到我對她的心意。

extra 額外的
a hint of my affection 一絲絲的心意

三明治以鮪魚
沙拉為基礎

- Tuna melt is one of the most **typical** American sandwiches. Based on tuna salad, it is constituted of layers of **lettuce** and cheese.

- 鮪魚三明治可説是最典型的美式三明治之一。三明治以鮪魚沙拉為基礎,再加上一層層的萵苣起士。

typical 典型的
lettuce 萵苣

蘋果派讓沮喪的心情平復、玉米麵包好吃的秘訣

MP3 022

■ I hate exams. **Finance** is absolutely devastating. After I stepped out of the classroom, I felt that I was gonna **collapse**.

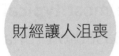
財經讓人沮喪

■ 我恨考試。財經真是讓我沮喪。走出教室的時候，我覺得我要崩潰了。

finance 財經
collapse 崩潰

■ Anyway, the hot tea in my hand is fixing my exam **anxiety**, and that's nice. I smell something very **fragrant**, is that cinnamon?

熱茶安撫了
焦躁的心

■ 不管啦,至少這杯熱茶安撫了我因考試而焦躁的心。我好像聞到什麼很香的味道,是肉桂嗎?

anxiety 焦躁
fragrant 芳香的

■ There he is, Alex is **grinning** and holding a **plate**. What is that? It's an apple pie! I can't believe this, did he make it himself? Let me have a bite first... hmmm!

艾力克斯帶
的蘋果派

■ 噢,艾力克斯帶著微笑現身了,他拿著個盤子。那是什麼?是個蘋果派耶!該不會是他自己做的吧?我簡直不敢相信。先來吃吃看吧!

grin 咧嘴笑
plate 盤子

■ After I had a few conversations with some girls, I headed back to the dining room for some snacks. On the table, aside from canapés and cocktail shrimp, I **spotted** cornbread.

■ 所以在我跟幾個女孩聊天後,我回到飯廳去拿點心。在放著吐司小點和蝦子酒杯的桌上,我發現了玉米麵包。

spot 發現了

■ I grabbed one and returned to the inner room. However, my step **paused** as I bit into the bread. It was super **moist** and fragrant. "This is probably the best cornbread I have ever had."

■ 隨手抓了一個後,我轉身回到裡面的房間。然而,就在我咬下玉米麵包的同時,我停下腳步;玉米麵包濕潤且香氣四溢。「我想這是我吃過最好吃的玉米麵包耶。」

pause 暫停
moist 濕潤的

發酵奶是好吃的秘訣

- Then I saw Paula **silently arranging** the cornbread on the plate. I went close to her and asked if she had brought it, she said yes. "I – I added buttermilk. That's why it's so tasty."

- 接著我發現寶拉默默擺放著桌上的玉米麵包。我走過去問這是否是她帶來的,她給我肯定的答案。「我一我加了發酵奶,這就是好吃的秘訣。」

silently 默默地
arrange 安排

玉米仍是主食

- Since the country of America was discovered and later filled with European **immigrants**, corn has remained the main food resource for many local residents.

- 美洲是在被歐洲人發現後,才有移民來定居,因此對許多當地人而言,時至今日,玉米仍擔任大部分食物來源。

immigrant 移民

MP3 023

■ Cooking is not only a woman's thing; actually, it is a man's thing. How can a **delicate** little woman handle a pot of grilled juicy **tenderloin**, or flip a whole pizza dough overhead?

披薩麵團舉到頭上旋轉

■ 下廚不是女性的專利；說實話，這其實是件相當陽剛的事。一位纖細的小姐怎麼能抬起一整鍋炙燒多汁的梅花豬肉，或把披薩麵團舉到頭上旋轉？

delicate 纖細的
tenderloin 梅花豬肉

■ That **smoking-hot** Latin babe just told me that she had no interest in dudes that don't **take a step in the kitchen**, but she will see what I've got.

對不進廚房的
老兄沒興趣

■ 那位火辣的拉丁妞剛告訴我，她對不進廚房的老兄沒興趣，她很快就會見識到我的能耐了。

smoking-hot 火辣的
take a step in the kitchen 進廚房

■ Tortilla chips, I prefer blue; chopped **onions**, chopped tomatoes, ground beef, chili, cumin, coriander, plus a big pile of **shredded** cheese.

像山一樣高的
起士絲

■ 我偏愛藍玉米製成的脆片，洋蔥丁、番茄丁、牛絞肉、辣椒粉、茴香子、香菜、最後是像山一樣高的起士絲。

onion 洋蔥
shredded 切碎的

■ **Originated** in Mexico, Nachos are now a popular bar food all-over America ; there is no must-put in the recipe. Usually, onions, tomatoes and chili are the basic **ingredients**, on a layer of tortilla chips.

風靡全美的酒吧必點菜

■ 源起於墨西哥，焗烤玉米片現在是風靡全美的酒吧必點菜。沒有固定的食譜。基本上，洋蔥、番茄和辣椒是固定班底，底層是墨西哥玉米片

originate 源起於
ingredient 成分

■ Hm, I love the **aroma** of chili. **Chili** is my favorite. Jessica is a very understanding woman; we started to live together about one year ago.

聞到辣豆燉肉的味道

■ 嗯，我喜愛辣豆燉肉的味道了，那是我的最愛。潔西卡是個相當善解人意的女人，我們大約一年前開始住在一起。

aroma 香味
Chili 辣豆燉肉

■ This chili is good. The beef is **tender**, the black beans are soft, and the **broth** is slightly tangy and flavorful.

牛肉軟嫩且黑豆熟爛

■ 辣豆燉肉真好吃，牛肉軟嫩，黑豆熟爛，湯微酸且充滿鮮味，我就愛這一味。

tender 柔軟的
broth 高湯

■ I tell Jessica how **dumb** I was today, hoping she won't be upset. To my surprise, she just **refills** my bowl with chili and says, "Everything is gonna be alright."

盛滿另一碗辣豆燉肉

■ 我告訴潔西卡今天我幹的蠢事，暗自希望她不會發怒。出乎意料的是，她默默的幫我盛滿另一碗辣豆燉肉，並告訴我：「一切都會沒事的」。

dumb 蠢的；笨的
refill 盛滿

1 生活、娛樂、科技和交通

2 異國飲食和人文風情

3 教育、知識、學習

4 工作和金錢的使用

莎莎醬搭墨西哥玉米片的滋味、中東蔬菜球的外酥內軟

MP3 024

■ The **encounter** with Peter on my trip to New Mexico is like tortilla chips and salsa. We just can't help but finish the whole **package** of chips once opened.

都喜歡辣味的
莎莎醬

■ 在新墨西哥旅行時與彼得的邂逅就像墨西哥玉米片和莎莎醬。我們都喜歡辣味的莎莎醬,那跟墨西哥玉米片最對味,每次開一包脆片就吃到見底。

encounter 邂逅
package 包

酪梨醬也跟墨西哥玉米片合拍

- Guacamole is also a good **companion** for tortilla chips, but for some reason, the mildness **turns us off**.

- 酪梨醬也跟墨西哥玉米片合拍，但不知為何，那股溫吞的感覺沒辦法勾起我們的食慾。

companion 伴侶；夥伴
turn sb.off 使某人喪失興致

墨西哥玉米片和莎莎醬的刺激

- The south is vast, hot and dry. Sometimes I feel the heat is going to **defeat** me, but every time the **stimulation** of tortilla chips and salsa keeps me going.

- 南方地廣，天氣又熱又乾。有時候我覺得炎熱簡直要把我擊垮了，但每次墨西哥玉米片和莎莎醬的刺激總能拉我一把，讓我繼續旅行。

defeat 打敗；打倒
stimulation 刺激

■ Although these fried, sometimes baked crispy corn chips are popular in the States **from coast to coast**, in Asia they are mostly **recognized** as the brand "Doritos".

■ 雖然這道油炸或烘烤而成的脆餅在全美十分普及，在亞洲，大部分人的印象卻僅止於多力多滋。調味玉米片的確酷炫又刺激，但未調味的玉米片才能和莎莎醬及酪梨醬完美合拍。

from coast to coast 全國；境內
recognize 認出；辨識

■ Mandy started her maple syrup stand not long after I **joined** Farmer's market. She didn't speak much, but her smile **melted** me every time.

■ 曼蒂是在我加入這個農夫市集不久後開設她的楓糖漿攤位的，她話不多，但她的微笑每次都叫我融化。

join 加入
melt 融化

以物易物

■ With a **bunch** of spinach in hand, I walked toward her and asked if she'd like to have a **trade**. She smiled, quietly turned around and grabbed a Ziploc bag from her cooler.

■ 我拿了一把菠菜走向她,並問她想不想以物易物。她安靜地笑了笑,轉身拿出一個密封袋。

bunch 捆、束
trade 交易

蔬菜球
外皮酥脆

■ To my surprise, it was falafel. The falafel, **crunchy** outside and soft inside, was full of flavor. Then it hit me that it was just like Mandy – quiet outwardly but **passionate** inwardly.

■ 竟是中東蔬菜球。蔬菜球外皮酥脆,內餡軟糯,滋味深遠。我突然發現這就像曼蒂一外表冷淡,內心火熱。

crunchy 酥脆的
passionate 熱情的

炸脆餅小點就像印度七色彩虹、印度香料炒飯像辣椒炸彈般

MP3 025

在同家
新聞社上班

■ The **bustling** Bombay produces awesome people like James. We work for the same newspaper, and we always **dine in** good restaurants.

■ 雜沓的孟買市產生了像是 James 這樣的優秀人才。我們在同家新聞社上班,且常到不錯的餐廳約會。

bustling 雜沓的
dine in 在⋯用餐

泥濘街上的骯髒小販

■ He takes me to a filthy vendor on a **muddy** road. as I watch the vendor pouring some green water **over** fried puffy pastry shells stuffed with God knows what. Ew, I don't even want to get close to it.

■ 他帶我到一個位在泥濘街上的骯髒小販。邊看著小販老闆把某種綠色的液體潑到裡面塞了鬼才知道是什麼的炸球餅裡面。噁，我完全不想靠近。

muddy 泥濘的

豐富的滋味像一道印度七色彩虹

■ He says with a smile on his face. I make up my mind and bite into it — and the pastry cracks and **releases** the flavor, like a delicious Indian rainbow in my mouth.

■ 他微笑著説。我硬著頭皮一口咬下去，霎時，豐富的滋味在嘴裡碎裂開來，像一道印度七色彩虹。

release 釋放

117

■ As I see the pile of rice arriving, Joshua starts to **scoop** the chili-colored rice into his mouth. The next thing I know is definitely not the way of eating it, but the **burst** of spices flavor on my tongue, like a spicy bomb.

■ 當我看到那堆如山高的炒飯上桌時，約書亞便開始將嫣紅色的炒飯舀進嘴裡。接下來我只知道，不是吃的方式而是香料味道在舌尖爆開，像辣椒炸彈。

將嫣紅色的炒飯舀進嘴裡

scoop 用湯匙舀
burst 爆發

■ It even keeps **stinging** after I **swallow**. "The water won't help, and we enjoy that."

■ 甚至在我嚥下之後，舌尖還感到陣陣刺痛。喝水也沒用，我們就愛這一味。

舌尖還感到陣陣刺痛

sting 刺、螫
swallow 吞嚥

■ He **reclines** at the table, with one hand throwing over-spiced fried rice into his mouth **unceasingly**. This chicken biriyani is certainly too spicy! Yet the man sitting in front of me enjoying this food makes my heart beat.

> 印度炒飯明顯是太辣了

■ 他輕鬆隨意的倚在桌邊，一隻手不間斷地將超辣的炒飯丟進嘴裡。這道印度炒飯明顯是太辣了！但這位坐在我對面，享受著佳餚的男士卻讓我心跳加速。

recline 斜倚
unceasingly 不停地

■ Like most Indian dishes, biriyani **is composed of** basmati rice cooked with many **different** spices.

> 使用相當多的香料

■ 就如同大多數的印度菜一樣，香料炒飯使用相當多的香料。

be composed of 由…組成
different 不同的

青木瓜沙拉上的蟹腳、冰火菠蘿油上的奶油魅力

 MP3 026

- The **crushed** crab in our salad made Dan and I scared. Language barriers in Thailand mattered. Dan and I met in the **hostel** the first night I arrived in Bangkok.

沙拉中搗碎的
螃蟹

- 我們沙拉中搗碎的螃蟹使我和丹飽受驚嚇。在泰國這裡語言障礙真的有影響。丹和我是在我抵達曼谷的第一晚，在青年旅社認識的。

crushed 搗碎的
hostel 青年旅館

■ However, our biggest **crises** happened the very next day: this dish of green papaya salad in front of us. I could still see the uncrushed leg of crab with its fur on it.

面前這盤青木瓜沙拉

■ 然而，巨大的危機第二天就發生了，也就是我們面前這盤青木瓜沙拉。我還看得到一隻沒被搗碎的蟹腳耶。

crises 危機

■ Was it raw or cooked? We had no **clue**. Yet, to my surprise, Dan moved **forward** and took a bite. "If I'm poisoned, at least I saved your life." He joked.

蟹腳上還有毛

■ 蟹腳上還有毛。這是生的還是熟的啊？我們沒有半點頭緒。然而，丹卻出乎意料的決定率先動筷。「如果我被毒死了，至少我還救了妳一命。」他開玩笑的說。

clue 線索
forward 向前；在前

1 生活、娛樂、科技和交通

2 異國飲食和人文風情

3 教育、知識、學習

4 工作和金錢的使用

121

- This is an **iconic** salad for Thailand. The combination of green papaya salad is unlimited. For the base, fish sauce, coconut sugar, lemon juice, garlic paste and red pepper are **critical**.

- 這是一道泰國指標性的沙拉,其組合有無限多種可能。以基底來說,魚露、椰糖、檸檬汁、蒜頭和朝天椒是必須的。

iconic 指標性的
critical 重要的

- Who can reject butter, ever? But for my own good and to **keep in shape**, I eat it very **moderately**.

- 誰能抗拒奶油的魅力呢?但為了我的健康和身材著想,我很克制。

keep in shape 保持身材
moderately 適度地

■ When I see people on the street biting and **savoring** their pineapple bun with butter, I'm like "wow...", especially when it is Gina. She eats **like no one else**.

大啖冰火
菠蘿油

■ 當我看到人們當街大啖冰火菠蘿油時，我常不禁發出「哇…」的感嘆，尤其是吉娜。她品嘗美食的模樣獨樹一幟。

savor 品嘗
like no one else 有自己的風格

■ I started going out with her, and most of the time, we go to the pineapple bun **vendor**. Seriously, with a bun like this and Yuanyang **in hand**, who can ask for more?

配上一杯
鴛鴦奶茶

■ 我開始跟她出雙入對，大部分時間，我們會光顧冰火菠蘿油的小販。說真的，有美食在手，配上一杯鴛鴦奶茶，夫復何求？

vendor 小販
in hand 手握

123

日本關東煮超便利、玉子燒帶出鄉愁感

MP3 027

■ In Japan, convenience stores run 24/7. It is super easy to get a snack or drink in the **dead of night**, especially when it is in walking **distance**.

便利商店全年無休

■ 在日本，便利商店是 24 小時營業的，全年無休。要在大半夜買個零食或飲料超方便，尤其是走路就會到。

dead of night 大半夜
distance 距離

- I love fish balls and cabbage rolls, whereas Kaori likes daikon and mushrooms. We meet at a 7-11 on the corner of the street, and soon two bowls of **steaming** hot oden **packed** soup are in our hands.

喜歡魚丸和
高麗菜卷

- 我喜歡魚丸和高麗菜卷，香織則是白蘿蔔和香菇的愛好者。我們在街角的 7-11 碰面，很快的，我們手裡便各自捧著一碗裝滿關東煮的熱湯。

steaming 冒著蒸氣的
packed 裝滿…的

- Holding a bowl of soup like this is as **comfy** as lying under a fluffy blanket. In truth having Kaori here is what makes the Oden truly enjoyable.

就像窩在
軟綿綿的被窩
裡一樣舒服

- 像這樣捧著一碗湯就像窩在軟綿綿的被窩裡一樣舒服。不過再怎麼說，香織還是讓這一切美味起來的決定性因素。

comfy 是 comfortable 的口語

既甜又鹹

- It is **odd** to have a sweet scrambled egg, isn't it? Actually, it's sweet yet salty.

- 甜煎蛋聽起來很怪，對吧？事實上，是既甜又鹹。

odd 奇怪的；怪異的

玉子燒那熟悉的滋味和外觀

- Sumito and I grew up in the same neighborhood. We soon moved to a bigger city. The familiar taste and texture of tamagoyaki somehow eases our **homesickness** in the bustling urban environment. No matter how the world changes, we are not alone.

- 純人和我從小一起長大，我們上同一所小學、初中、高中。我們很快就搬到城市生活。玉子燒那熟悉的滋味和外觀不知怎地一解我們的鄉愁。不論世界怎麼變，我們都不孤單。

homesickness 鄉愁

■ Whenever I bite into a juicy tamagoyaki, with its two **opposite** flavors dancing on top of my tongue so **harmoniously**, I can't help but close my eyes and think of my childhood.

（兩種味道在舌尖完美融合並跳躍著）

■ 每當我大口咬下多汁的玉子燒時，兩種相反的味道在舌尖完美融合並跳躍著，總讓我不禁閉上雙眼，並讓這股味道將我帶回到兒時。

opposite 相反的
harmoniously 和諧地

■ It's not overly sweet, he claims, yet the **chunkiness** of sugar is in every bite, along with the aroma of soy sauce which is brought out by the salt.

（每口都吃得到砂糖的脆脆顆粒）

■ 他說不會太甜，但是每口都吃得到砂糖的脆脆顆粒，並嘗得到被鹽帶出的醬油香味。

chunkiness 酥脆感

1 生活、娛樂、科技和交通

2 異國飲食和人文風情

3 教育、知識、學習

4 工作和金錢的使用

127

MP3 028

■ I **treasure** the customs and **moral** values, which teach me to respect the ancestors and give thanks for every piece of food. For young people in our generation, this is definitely not common.

重視習俗和
道德價值

■ 我很重視習俗和道德價值，例如尊重先祖、對每一份食物感懷在心等等。對我們這一代的年輕人而言，要維持這樣的想法相當不容易。

treasure 重視；珍視
moral 道德的

■ We both like **azuki bean rice cake**, fried or baked. Our grandparents are old enough to make the best rice cakes, and we enjoy them every year. The most important thing in life is the people one shares the moment with.

都很喜歡
紅豆年糕

■ 我們都很喜歡紅豆年糕，不管是炸的還是烤的。外公、外婆經驗老到，他們做的年糕是最棒的，而我們每年都享用到他們的手藝。人生中最重要的事情，莫過於那些與我們分享重要時刻的人們。

azuki bean rice cake 紅豆年糕

■ Made with mashed rice and steamed afterward, rice cake has been a **traditional** food for new year throughout Korea, Japan and China for centuries.

搗爛的米蒸煮
而成的年糕

■ 由搗爛的米蒸煮而成的年糕，是韓國、日本及中國好幾世紀以來的傳統年節料理。各國料理年糕的方式各異其趣。

traditional 傳統的

1
生活、娛樂、科技和交通

2
異國飲食和人文風情

3
教育、知識、學習

4
工作和金錢的使用

■ My darling is here! I can't believe this! I get in his car and there's another **surprise**: a gift box! Wow, that's my man...Luc took me to a nice restaurant, and ordered chicken satay.

■ 這不是我的達令嗎！我真不敢相信！上了車，那兒有另一個驚喜等著我：一個禮物盒！哇，不愧是我的男人。路克帶我到一間不錯的餐館，並點了雞肉沙嗲串。

surprise 驚喜

點了雞肉
沙嗲串

■ I doubted because I've never tried a chicken satay. There it comes, five flat chicken breast on the **skewers**, nice and neat. And there's a separate dish of satay sauce, which is dark brown and a little bit cloudy.

■ 我挺懷疑的，因為我沒吃過雞肉沙嗲串。上菜了，五片串在烤肉串上的雞胸肉整齊又優雅的放在那兒；另一個盤子上放著沙嗲醬，顏色深棕且有點混濁。

skewer 烤肉串

雞胸肉整齊
又優雅

■ I look up to Luc, **hesitantly**. Luc nods his head and tells me to **dig in**. Undoubtedly, everything's tasty.

食物棒呆了

■ 我遲疑地抬頭看著路克，他則點點頭示意我開動。無庸置疑的，食物棒呆了。

hesitantly 猶疑地；遲疑地
dig in 開動

■ Satay is an Indonesian dish, which much **admired** among Asian countries. Satay refers to both the meat and the sauce. Chicken, beef, pork or even tofu can be used as **protein** in this dish.

沙嗲串燒是
一道印尼菜

■ 沙嗲串燒是一道印尼菜，在亞洲各國間相當有人氣。「沙嗲」一詞可用於指稱沙嗲串燒及沙嗲醬。雞、牛、豬或甚至豆腐都可用在這道菜上。

admire 仰慕；喜歡
protein 蛋白質

皮蛋豆腐的奇遇、讓人眼睛為之一亮的蘿蔔糕

 MP3 029

- Being known as thousands year egg or **preserved** egg, century egg is made by preserving duck eggs. It is black, half-**transparent** in the white, dark and gooey in the yolk.

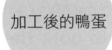

加工後的鴨蛋

- 皮蛋也被稱為千年蛋或醃漬蛋,是一種加工後的鴨蛋。皮蛋是 黑色的,蛋白呈半透明狀、蛋黃是流動的暗黑色。

preserve 封存;保存
transparent 透明的

點皮蛋豆腐

■ But hey! That's Judy! She actually has lunch in this noodle **stand** often as well, and she also orders **century egg and tofu**.

■ 嘿！那不是茱蒂嗎？她還滿常跟我在同一間麵攤吃午餐的，而且她也都會點皮蛋豆腐。

stand 小吃攤；小攤販
century egg and tofu 皮蛋豆腐

很樂意跟她分享皮蛋豆腐

■ Oh, I see her reaching in her pocket for coins... does she **happen to** be **short of** money for the moment? This is my chance! I'd love to share my century egg and tofu with her!

■ 喔，我看到她把手放在口袋裡掏錢了…是不是剛好沒帶夠錢啊？我的機會來了！我很樂意跟她分享皮蛋豆腐！

happen to 剛好
short of 少了...

133

- Roaring scooters make the foreigner like Peter a little bit lost. I'd say that if you grow up in the **jungle**, you'll know how to get along with the beasts.

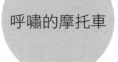
呼嘯的摩托車

- 呼嘯的摩托車讓像是彼得這樣的外國人有點迷失。彼得問。這個嘛，我會說若你在叢林長大，你總得學著跟野獸相處。

jungle 熱帶叢林

- I lead Peter into a traditional breakfast shop. "It's **shabby**, kind of." He frowns, following my step reluctantly. Don't judge a book by its cover is my motto, and I think it's time for Peter to learn it.

到一家傳統
早餐店

- 我帶彼得到一家傳統早餐店，「有點髒。」他皺眉，不情願地跟上我的腳步。不要以貌取人是我的座右銘，我想是讓彼得學習這句話的時候了。

shabby 簡陋的

■ Hot, crispy daikon cake is my favorite breakfast. Peter tastes his first bite carefully, but soon his eyes **shine forth** and he starts to **devour** the cake.

熱呼呼、硬脆的蘿蔔糕

■ 熱呼呼、硬脆的蘿蔔糕是我最愛的早餐。彼得小心翼翼地咬下第一口,突然眼睛一亮,並開始狼吞虎嚥的吃掉蘿蔔糕。

shine forth 閃亮;亮起
devour 吞噬;狼吞虎嚥

■ "You surely have a taste for food." Peter **acclaims**, cheerfully savoring the daikon cake like it was a lobster. Once you enter the jungle, never think of leaving without a **scratch**.

眼前的蘿蔔糕是條龍蝦

「你對食物很有品味嘛。」彼得讚美道,歡欣鼓舞的樣子好似眼前的蘿蔔糕是條龍蝦。一旦進了叢林,就別妄想毫髮無傷地離開。

acclaim 讚美;讚嘆
scratch 擦傷;刮痕

1 生活、娛樂、科技和交通

2 異國飲食和人文風情

3 教育、知識、學習

4 工作和金錢的使用

法國韃靼的料理、熱巧克力的魅力

■ The egg, with its cooked white and raw yolk, looks so **enticing**. It sits on a bed of beef tartare, **garnished** with a stem of scallion.

> 生蛋穩坐在
> 牛肉上

■ 蛋白熟透、蛋黃卻還生生的雞蛋看起來引人食慾。生蛋穩坐在牛肉上，並以一條細蔥裝飾。

enticing 引人食慾的
garnish 裝飾

瞧瞧那流淌而下的蛋汁

■ He **moves away** the scallion stem, and carefully cuts into the yolk. Look at that liquid **dripping** over the tartare! It looks so yummy.

■ 湯瑪斯拿開細蔥，並小心的切開蛋黃。瞧瞧那流淌而下的蛋汁！看起來真美味。

move away 拿開
drip 滴落

蛋汁突然噴射而出

■ I take up the knife to cut mine, but just as the **blade** touches the yolk, it suddenly **splashes** out! Thomas looks stunned for a second, but we both burst out laughing together immediately.

■ 我拿起餐刀準備切我的蛋，但就在刀鋒碰到蛋黃的那一刻，蛋汁突然噴射而出！湯瑪斯愣了一秒，接著我們兩個開始爆笑起來。

blade 刀鋒
splash 噴；濺；灑

- Every time I have a **fight** with Jean, I come here. "Lily of the Lake" is the name of the coffee shop, but I don't drink coffee. I choose **hot chocolate** every time.

- 每次我跟約翰有不愉快，我就會到這裡來。「湖邊的百合」是這家咖啡廳的名字。我不喝咖啡，我喝熱巧克力。

fight 爭執、口角
hot chocolate 熱巧克力

- I find **shelter** here. Whenever my lips touch the sticky liquid, a special chemical simultaneously grabs me and throws me into another **zone**.

- 在這裡，我找到庇蔭處。每當我的嘴唇碰到那黏稠的液體時，一種特別的感覺立即攫住我，並將我拋入另一個時空。

shelter 收容所
zone 領域、地區

138

混合著苦澀與香甜的鹹味

■ The salty **mix** with the bitter-sweet chocolate taste is like tear drops **rolling down** my throat.

■ 那混合著苦澀與香甜的鹹味，就如眼淚般簌簌滑下我的喉嚨。

mix 混合
rolling down 滑下

法式熱巧克力又濃又稠

■ Hot chocolate varies from region to region, country to country. French hot chocolate is usually considered very thick and creamy. Instead of using chocolate powder, they **melt chunks** of chocolate; instead of water, they use milk.

■ 熱巧克力會因地區及國家而有許多不同的表現。法式熱巧克力普遍被認為是又濃又稠；法國人用塊狀巧克力取代沖泡巧克力粉，並用鮮奶取代白開水。

melt 融化
chunk 塊

昂貴的柳橙鴨、焗烤火腿乳酪吐司

■ **Soft music**, burning candles and the **chatters** of glasses — I have finally taken a girl to a restaurant like this! It doesn't matter how much it costs... well, actually, it does.

> 輕音樂、搖曳的燭火還有玻璃杯的碰撞聲

■ 輕音樂、搖曳的燭火還有玻璃杯的碰撞聲—我終於成功的帶著女孩子上這種餐館了！價錢不是重點……噢，沒有啦！

soft music 輕音樂
chatter 聲響；震動

■ I've been saving and living poor just for this meal. The waiter is kind enough to hand a menu without price tags to my partner; that's wise, because the price here almost gives me an **ulcer**.

這價錢幾乎要讓我得胃潰瘍了

■ 其實為了吃這頓，我已經省吃儉用存錢了好一陣子。服務生真好，他給我的女伴的菜單是沒有標價錢的。真精明，因為這價錢幾乎要讓我得胃潰瘍了。

ulcer 潰瘍

■ Excellent, they have authentic French cuisine. Cloe is a **foodie**; I will let her order to show my respect. We have duck à l'orange and rose wine. How romantic!

點了柳橙鴨和粉紅酒

■ 好極了，他們有正統法國菜。克蘿伊很會品嘗美食，還是讓她點餐以示尊重吧。我們點了柳橙鴨和粉紅酒。真浪漫呀！

foodie 老饕

法國菜中的翹楚

■ No matter where its origin was, Duck à l'orange is **absolutely** a **signature** dish now in France and all-over the world.

■ 不論其出身地為何，柳橙鴨絕對是法國菜中的翹楚，且已遍傳全球。

absolutely 絕對地
signature 簽名；簽署

點了焗烤火腿乳酪吐司

■ Feeling pretty proud of my French **progress**, I order Un croque-madame, s'il vous plait in French, of course, a dish I desperately need after an **exhausted** morning class.

■ 對自己法語進步速度感到相當有自信，我點了焗烤火腿乳酪吐司，一道在令人感到筋疲力盡的早上課程後迫切需要的菜餚。

progress 進步
exhausted 筋疲力盡的

- Unluckily, something **strikes** me the next second and **destroys** my pride completely: I forgot to bring the money! I can't believe this is happening to me.

**徹底摧毀
我自信心**

- 不幸的是，下一秒便發生了徹底摧毀我自信心的慘事：我忘記帶錢了！真不敢相信這種事發生在我身上！

strike 擊中；使…有印象
destroy 摧毀

- Now, savoring the creamy, egg-**soaked** toast, I feel that something more than friendship is **fermenting** - maybe something called love.

**流淌著蛋汁的
焗烤火腿乳酪
吐司**

- 現在，品嘗著香濃、流淌著蛋汁的焗烤火腿乳酪吐司，我感到友情以外的某個元素正在發酵。也許，是愛情吧。

soak 浸泡
ferment 發酵

1 生活、娛樂、科技和交通

2 異國飲食和人文風情

3 教育、知識、學習

4 工作和金錢的使用

像食療般的炸魚薯條、農舍派的香氣

MP3 032

■ As a **foreign** student, London is not very friendly to me. It rains all the time. What causes me **melancholy** is not only weather, but also food. I miss hot food, fresh vegetables and savory soups.

想念熱騰騰的飯

■ 對我這個留學生而言,倫敦並不友善;這裡老是在下雨。讓我憂鬱的還不只是天氣,還有食物。我想念熱騰騰的飯、新鮮蔬菜和滋味馥郁的湯品。

foreign 外國人
melancholy 憂鬱;哀傷

■ One day, Loran caught me after class and **asked me out**. Loran is **born and raised** in London, but he doesn't possess the arrogance that some British people have.

■ 一天，羅倫在下課後約我出去。羅倫是土生土長的倫敦人，但他沒有一些英國人抱持的傲慢。

> 土生土長的倫敦人

ask sb. out 邀約某人
born and raised 土生土長的

■ At the end of the day, he told me to try some fish and chips. If it was not for the day, I'd have **rejected**. Nevertheless, the fresh fried fish and chips were not only crispy, but also refreshing.

■ 最後，羅倫帶我嘗試炸魚薯條。若不是當天太愉快，我一定會拒絕的。然而，剛炸好的炸魚薯條不僅酥脆，更是令我耳目一新。

> 剛炸好的炸魚薯條不僅酥脆

reject 拒絕

■ I never knew that **junk food** could be so good! "The **secret** is salt and malt vinegar."

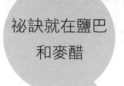

■ 我從不知道垃圾食物是這麼美味！「祕訣就在鹽巴和麥醋。」

junk food 垃圾食物
secret 祕訣

■ In a blink of time, my front yard is paved with snow. I have to park my truck in the garage. The snow causes trouble: vision is **blurred**, tires slide, all kinds of **dreadful** accidents take place.

■ 很快地，前院就積滿了雪，我必須把卡車停到車庫裡去。雪總是帶來麻煩，比如視線不清啦、輪胎打滑啦，什麼意外都會發生。

blur 使模糊
dreadful 可怕的；嚇人的

■ Still, **on this kind of day**, good things happen. For example, making **cottage pie**!

烤個農舍派

■ 這種日子還是會有好事的，例如說烤個農舍派。

on this kind of day 這種日子
cottage pie 農舍派

■ So I cook up the beef, **simmer** it in tomato sauce, and top the pot with mashed potato. The fragrance of meat **circulates** in the air as the pie sits tranquilly in the oven.

將牛肉在番茄糊中燉煮

■ 於是我開始烹煮牛肉，將牛肉在番茄糊中燉煮，並在鍋頂鋪上馬鈴薯泥。當派安安靜靜地在烤箱中烘烤時，屋裡漸漸充滿了肉煮熟的香氣。

simmer 煨；燉
circulate 流通；流轉

米派之遇、鮭魚蒔蘿在奶油海裡

MP3 033

- Since the first day I arrived in Helsinki, I've been **enduring** the food they have here. Sour bread, **tasteless** crackers – not a single thing I have here can possibly be called tasty.

酸味麵包、食之無味的餅乾

- 自從我第一天到達赫爾辛基，我就一直在忍受芬蘭的食物。酸味麵包、食之無味的餅乾，沒一樣食物會讓我覺得好吃。

endure 忍耐；忍受
tasteless 無味的

■ Sarah **treated** me with fried sausages, freshly **tossed** green salad, and vanilla ice cream.

■ 莎拉招待我吃炒香腸、新鮮沙拉和香草冰淇淋。

招待我吃炒香腸、新鮮沙拉和香草冰淇淋

treat 招待
toss 拋；擲；甩

■ The next day, before I **departed for** the ferry, she treated me again with a wonderful breakfast: Karelian pastry. The pastry was warm, and I hadn't liked it since the first time I tasted it. However, warm Karelian pastry tasted **fluffy**, and the rice inside is creamy.

內餡的米飯也很綿密

■ 次日，在我出發去搭渡輪前，她又再次招待我豐盛的早餐：芬蘭米派。米派是溫熱的。從我第一次吃到這種派起，我就不曾對它有好感。然而溫熱的米派卻嘗起來蓬鬆可口，內餡的米飯也很綿密。

depart for 出發前往⋯
fluffy 蓬鬆的

混合普通麵粉
與裸麥粉

- In Finland, rye is used in every pastry: bread, crackers, **etc**. To make Karelian pastry, first mix all purpose flour and **rye flour**.

- 在芬蘭，裸麥（黑麥）廣泛的被運用在麵粉製品中，比如麵包、餅乾等。要製作米派，需先混合普通麵粉與裸麥粉。

etc 等等（前加逗號）
rye flour 裸麥粉

交換過
隻字片語

- Tonight my host is a guy named Jouni. We only **exchanged** a few words online, and now I'm going to **spend the night** with a stranger, plus he is a man.

- 今晚我的宿主是一位名叫尤尼的男性；我們僅僅在網路上交換過隻字片語，然後我就要跟這個陌生人共度一宿還是個男人。

exchange 交換
spend the night 過夜

■ To my **relief**, Jouni has a nice **personality**. Being in his tiny apartment feels relaxed. He prepared salmon chowder for me.

準備了鮭魚蒔蘿濃湯

■ 尤尼是個好人真讓我鬆了口氣,迷你的公寓也讓我很放鬆。他為我準備了鮭魚蒔蘿濃湯。

relief 放鬆;慰藉
personality 個性;人格

■ "It's dill. We love dill here in **Sweden**." The soup is **creamy and warm**. Flakes of dill are like cute little grass in a white ocean. The more I sip on the soup, the less nervous I am.

像可愛的綠草

■ 「蒔蘿。我們瑞典人可喜歡蒔蘿了。」這道湯又濃郁又溫暖,一片片蒔蘿在奶油海裡像可愛的綠草。

Sweden 瑞典人
creamy and warm 濃郁又溫暖

布魯塞爾格子鬆餅、焦糖煎餅

MP3 034

■ It's hard to neglect waffle houses on the streets of Brussels. They are everywhere. I **am** not **crazy about** sugary sweets, but **it won't harm** to have a taste of the country.

要忽視一間一間的鬆餅屋相當難

■ 走在布魯塞爾街上,要忽視一間一間的鬆餅屋相當難;它們無所不在。我並不特別喜歡甜點,但淺嘗幾口倒是無傷大雅。

be crazy about 不喜歡某事／物
it won't harm 也不會怎麼樣

■ Since there are so many, I want to have **the real deal**. "I'd suggest that we skip those fancy decorations and go for pure **genuineness**."

不想踩雷

■ 鬆餅屋這麼多，我可不想踩雷。「我建議我們跳過那些華麗的配料，吃原味就好。」

the real deal 好東西；真貨
genuineness 真實；真正

■ Hot waffles are **delivered** to our hands. The sugar is caramelized perfectly on the surface. With just one bite, the soft-chewiness has **blown my mind**.

砂糖在表面形成完美的焦糖層

■ 熱呼呼的格子鬆餅送到我們手上了，砂糖在表面形成完美的焦糖層。我才吃一口，那軟綿又有嚼勁的口感立刻叫我大吃一驚。

deliver 送到
blow one's mind away 使某人大開眼界

- Waffles **are identified by** their square-shaped surface. Different from pancakes, these little pastries are **crispier** and easier to hold in hand.

小型糕點較酥脆

- 格子鬆餅因其一格一格的外型而擁有高辨識度。不同於美式熱鬆糕，這些小型糕點較酥脆，也較易用手取食。

be identified by 以…來辨認
crispy 酥脆的

- This thin, sticky cookie-waffle like dessert is **addictive**. My favorite way of eating stroopwafel is, **undoubtedly**, place it on top of a steaming hot coffee.

放在熱氣蒸騰的咖啡

- 這片薄薄黏黏、像餅乾又像鬆餅的甜點令人上癮。我最愛的焦糖煎餅吃法，不用說，當然是放在熱氣蒸騰的咖啡上。

addictive 令人上癮的
undoubtedly 無庸置疑地

■ After a while, the heat **melts down** the caramel inside the pastry. That's when I take it up, **appreciate** its beauty for a few seconds, and eat it.

> 熱氣便會融化中間的焦糖夾層

■ 不消片刻，熱氣便會融化中間的焦糖夾層，這便是我拿起煎餅的時機；我會先花幾秒欣賞誘人的煎餅，接著一口吃下。

melt down 融化
appreciate 欣賞；感激

■ This is a **world-famous** Dutch dessert. It is made with two layers of thin wafers with caramel filling. The caramel is **stiff** at room temperature.

> 聞名世界的荷蘭甜點

■ 這是一個聞名世界的荷蘭甜點，由兩片輕薄的煎餅中間夾著焦糖製成。焦糖在室溫下為固態。

world-famous 聞名世界的
stiff 僵硬的；僵直的

1 生活、娛樂、科技和交通

2 異國飲食和人文風情

3 教育、知識、學習

4 工作和金錢的使用

155

俄國羅宋湯、奧地利丹麥麵包

■ Andrew is a good friend of mine, and he **introduces** many things in Russia to me. Today, he invites me to do some **research** in his house. Andrew prepared traditional borscht and sour cream dill roll-ups.

傳統羅宋湯和酸奶蒔蘿卷

■ 安德魯是我的一位好友,他為我打開了認識俄羅斯的大門,我對此心懷感謝。這天,他邀請我到他家去做些研究。安德魯準備了傳統羅宋湯和酸奶蒔蘿卷。

introduce A to B 將 A 介紹給 B
research 研究

■ For me, everything is new. In order to be polite, even though I'm so tempted by all the good food, I do not just **dive into** the **delicacies** on the table.

仍把持住自己

■ 對我而言，一切都是那麼新奇，然而為了保持禮貌，儘管美食當前，我仍把持住自己，沒有立刻忘情大吃。

dive into 開動
delicacy 美食

■ "Here, try it with some more sour cream." **A pile of** sour cream is scooped into my bowl. I take a breath and take a spoon. "It is so **flavorful**!" I exclaim.

把一大匙酸奶舀到我的碗裡

■ 「加點酸奶一起品嚐吧！」說完就把一大匙酸奶舀到我的碗裡。我深深的吸了一口氣，接著吃了一匙。「好有滋味呀！」。

a pile of 一疊；一堆
flavorful 美味的

■ Borscht **originates** in Ukraine, and it has become famous in East Europe **as time goes on**. The basic ingredients for borscht are beets, salt, sugar and lemon juice.

以牛肉湯為基底

■ 羅宋湯起源自烏克蘭,並隨時間推移漸漸流行到東歐地區。羅宋湯的基本原料為甜菜、鹽、糖和檸檬汁。在俄國,羅宋湯通常以牛肉湯為基底,胡蘿蔔、馬鈴薯及菠菜是常見的湯料。

originate 源自
as time goes on 隨著時間過去

■ "I **look right into** her eyes, trying to find some **sympathy** there. She looks back at me and suddenly smiles. "Here, have a Danish pastry."

吃個丹麥麵包

■ 我望進她眼裡,想從那兒找到一絲同情。她回望我,並突然微笑起來。「喂,吃個丹麥麵包吧。」

look right into 直接望進
sympathy 憐憫心

■ That's fishy. "Danish pastry doesn't come from Denmark. They just **fake it**. Who cares? It tastes good. That's what counts." She suddenly leans forward and gives me a kiss. I guess she's got that spell on me.

麵包好吃，這就夠了

■ 「丹麥麵包不是從丹麥來的，只是以訛傳訛。但，誰在乎呢？麵包好吃，這就夠了。」她突然傾身向前吻了我，我想我中了她的魔咒了。

fake sth.（假裝做）某事

■ Despite its name, Danish pastry actually came from Austria and **flourished** in Denmark. In Europe, there are roughly two kinds of bread: thin bread and rich bread.

在丹麥發揚光大

■ 其名饒富興味，丹麥麵包其實源自奧地利，而在丹麥發揚光大。在歐洲，麵包可粗略分為兩種：「瘦麵包」和「滋養麵包」。

flourish 發揚

1 生活、娛樂、科技和交通

2 異國飲食和人文風情

3 教育、知識、學習

4 工作和金錢的使用

MP3 036

■ As far as I know, German dudes are stubborn (comparatively), **eloquent** and extremely proud of their culture. I think it's strange, but I'**m drawn to** their men and their culture.

對自己的文化極端自負

■ 目前為止，我認為德國人相當頑固（比較起來啦！），好辯且對自己的文化極端自負。對此，相當神奇的是，我無法否認自己受其吸引。

eloquent 辯才無礙的
be drawn to 受⋯吸引

160

■ Being pen pals for 6 months, I'm paying Ben a visit. He told me that **hot dogs** in the United States aren't equal to **Frankfurter sausage**.

■ 當了六個月的筆友後，我拜訪了班。他告訴我美國熱狗不等同法蘭克福香腸。

> 我美國熱狗不等同法蘭克福香腸

hot dog 熱狗
Frankfurter sausage 法蘭克福香腸

■ The restaurant is an all-you can- eat buffet. My eyes are wide open when I **spot** dozens of different sausages lying there, with sauerkraut and pickled cabbage, all those mouth-watering **morsels**.

■ 他帶我去一家吃到飽餐廳，看到十幾二十種的香腸，我眼睛睜得老大。還有德國酸菜、醃漬高麗菜等等，各種各樣令人口水直流的美味。

> 還有德國酸菜、醃漬高麗菜

spot 發現；看到
morsel 塊（此指菜餚）

■ Germany **is known as** a country of "sausage and beer". Truly, sausage alone is widely **consumed** in Germany.

■ 德國是一個以「香腸和啤酒」聞名的國家。的確，香腸不僅在德國境內銷量高，也風靡德國的臨近歐洲國家及美國。

is known as 以…聞名
consume 消耗

■ Every family in **Poland** cooks Flaki, but somehow, the overwhelming smell of it is just **disgusting** to me.

■ 每個波蘭家庭都會烹調牛肚湯，但不知為何，牛肚湯詭異的味道讓我覺得噁心。

Poland 波蘭
disgusting 令人感到噁心的

- Ola is my girlfriend. We started **seeing each other** a few weeks ago and she comes to my place **frequently**. Despite the fact that I dislike Flaki, she cooks it all the time.

老是在煮
這道湯

- 歐拉是我的女友,我們幾週前開始交往後,她便很常到我家來。雖然我不喜歡,她卻老是在煮這道湯。

seeing each other 交往
frequently 頻繁地

- The strong **scent** of cattle tripe is **lingering** in the whole place: bedroom, bathroom, everywhere. I am irritated and I walk toward her angrily.

強烈臭味
在整個家縈
繞不去

- 烹煮牛肚的強烈臭味在整個家縈繞不去,臥室、廁所,到處都是。

scent 氣味
lingering 縈繞不去的

MP3 037

■ Oh boy, the gorgeous woman waving at me inside must be Carrie. Thank God! She looks **in shape** and healthy. I **hop in** the store in a hurry.

> 看起來
> 身材勻稱

■ 感謝上天！她看起來身材勻稱且健康。我急急忙忙走進店內。

in shape 身材良好
hop in 急急忙忙進入⋯

■ I notice that Carrie already ordered a plate of churros and two cups of chocolate. "You like churros?" I asked, **trembling** with **excitement**.

■ 發現卡莉已經點了一盤吉拿棒和兩杯熱巧克力。「你喜歡吉拿棒嗎？」我因為興奮而顫抖著問道。

> 點了一盤吉拿棒和兩杯熱巧克力

tremble 顫抖
excitement 興奮

■ "I do! Do you? I think it goes well with **bittersweet** chocolate." She chatters, with her beautiful finger **dipping** a churro in her cup.

■ 「喜歡啊！你呢？我覺得吉拿棒跟苦甜巧克力很搭。」她格格笑著說，一邊用她修長美麗的手指將吉拿棒浸入杯中的巧克力裡。

> 吉拿棒跟苦甜巧克力很搭

bittersweet 苦甜的
dipping 浸入

1 生活、娛樂、科技和交通

2 異國飲食和人文風情

3 教育、知識、學習

4 工作和金錢的使用

■ Churro is a Spanish fried pastry. The dough itself **resemble**s the one for donuts, but after it's fried, the center becomes **hollow**.

■ 吉拿棒是一種西班牙的油炸點心。生麵團跟甜甜圈的麵團十分相似，然而油炸後，吉拿棒中間會呈空心狀。

resemble 與…類似
hollow 中空的

■ I look closely to David's hands, trying to **record** the secret recipe of making this **knockout** tomato garlic bread.

■ 我仔細地盯著大衛的手，試著記下這道「驚世番茄大蒜麵包」的秘密配方。

record 紀錄
knockout 傑出的

■ The **lousy** weather pushed me out of the country. Spain; however, seems to be the **opposite**. Everything is so bright and warm.

■ 糟糕的天氣讓我出走。然而，西班牙就像另一個相反的國度：這裡的一切都是閃耀又溫暖的。

另一個相反的國度

lousy 糟糕的
opposite 相反的

■ "it's coming out of the oven!" David **cheer**s. The olive oil and tomato juice are glowing on the hot toast, and David is just the **shining star** of mine.

■「出爐囉！」大衛歡呼。橄欖油和番茄的汁液在熱呼呼的麵包上閃耀，而大衛則是我的亮麗巨星。

橄欖油和番茄的汁液

cheer 歡呼
shining star 閃亮巨星

奧地利薩赫蛋糕、俄國油炸包

■ "Jack, this is for you." Like a **tornado**, Natasha shows up in my classroom, lands a package of cake on my desk and departs. She always **makes my head spin**.

放了個蛋糕在桌子

■ 「傑克，這個給你。」娜塔莎像旋風一樣的出現在我的教室，放了個蛋糕在桌子上後又倏地離開。她總是搞得我暈頭轉向。

tornado 颶風
make one's head spin 令人暈頭轉向

喜歡她蛋糕的
大有人在

■ No matter how many times I tell her that I don't fancy sweets, she never stops giving out her **chef d'oevre**. Unlike me, many peers of mine are fans of Natasha's creations.

■ 不管我告訴她幾次我不愛甜食，她從未停止送我她的蛋糕作品。我的死黨們倒跟我不同，喜歡她蛋糕的大有人在。

chef d'oeuvre 大師之作

等著分一杯羹

■ I don't eat them and my classmates circle me like **scavenger** birds looking for a bite. I open the package, and there is a sachertorte. It's dark, chocolatey, and sweet **visually**.

■ 娜塔莎送我蛋糕的慣例讓我感到不舒服，我不吃蛋糕，而我的同學們總像禿鷹一樣環繞著我，等著分一杯羹。打開盒子，裡面是一個薩赫蛋糕。看起來黑嘛嘛的、很「巧克力」、一副很甜的樣子。

scavenger 清道夫
visually 視覺上地

■ I cut off an **edge** of sachertorte, expecting the **explosion** of a sugary bomb. To my surprise, the first thing I taste is bitterness.

接受砂糖炸彈的衝擊

■ 就在我一片片送出蛋糕之際，我突然靈光一閃：為什麼不自己吃一片呢？於是我切了蛋糕一角，預備接受砂糖炸彈的衝擊。令我驚訝的是，最先嘗到的味道卻是苦味。

edge 邊緣
explosion 爆炸

■ Being with Rose always makes me feel **comfortable**, I think she feels the same. "Hey, you have breakfast yet?" She suddenly asks, and **hesitantly** hands me a paper bag. It's Pirozhki!

裡面是油炸包

■ 跟蘿絲相處總讓我感到放鬆，我想她也有一樣的感覺。「嘿，你吃早餐了沒？」她突然問道，並遲疑地遞給我一個紙袋。裡面是油炸包！

comfortable 舒適的
hesitantly 遲疑地

■ This is a little bun with various fillings tucked inside. The bread is **stuffed**, **baked** and then fried.

烘烤後炸

■ 這是一種塞滿內餡的小麵包。這種麵包先填餡、烘烤最後油炸。

stuffed 填餡
baked 烘烤

■ It is a convenient snack or light meal, which can be served savory as well as sweet. The stuffing is almost **unlimited**: from meat, egg, rice and vegetables, to fresh or **cooked** fruit.

口味可鹹可甜

■ 這也是一種方便的點心或便餐，口味可鹹可甜。麵包內餡幾乎是沒有限制的：從肉類、蛋、米飯和蔬菜，到新鮮或煮過的水果。

unlimited 沒有限制的
cooked 煮過的

1 生活、娛樂、科技和交通

2 異國飲食和人文風情

3 教育、知識、學習

4 工作和金錢的使用

芬蘭肉桂捲、義大利冰淇淋凍糕

 MP3 039

■ My boyfriend is an instagramer. Whenever we order something in a café or a restaurant, he never **allow**s me to eat unless he has taken the **photo**s he wants.

是個 instagramer

■ 我的男友是個 instagramer 玩家，每次我們去咖啡館或上餐廳，他總要先拍夠照片才准我開吃。

allow 允許
photo 照片

- I **roll my eyes**. Come on! The food is getting cold! I'm sick of it. Finally, after he finishes his **photography**, I take a bite on my lovely cinnamon roll.

翻了個白眼

- 我翻了個白眼。拜託喔！食物都冷了！終於，他照完相了，而我得以大口咬下我的肉桂捲。

roll my eyes 翻了個白眼
photography 照相

- One of the reasons I like it is because of the hot, **sticky** cinnamon **icing on the top**. "The icing on the cake" totally works here.

蛋糕上的糖霜

- 我喜歡肉桂捲的原因之一，是因為上頭有溫熱、黏呼呼的肉桂糖霜。「蛋糕上的糖霜」是最棒的部分，此話不假。

sticky 黏呼呼的
icing on the top 糖霜在上頭

■ Lindsey is a loyal customer of our coffee shop. She comes in every morning, and that's how we got talking. "So you like to cook?" She looked surprised, even forgot to drink her **Macchiato**.

■ 莉西是我們咖啡廳的常客,她每天早上都來光顧,而這就是我們聊起來的契機。「所以你喜歡下廚呀?」她看起來很驚訝,甚至忘了喝她的焦糖瑪奇朵。

Macchiato 焦糖瑪奇朵

■ I promised to cook a complete Italian meal for her. Luckily, with some help from my friends, I managed to prepare an appetizer and the **entrées**.

■ 我承諾做一頓義式大餐給她吃。還好,因為幾位朋友的幫忙,我成功的做出了開胃菜和主餐。

entrées 主餐

問題出在冰淇
淋凍糕

- Now, the thing is the **semifreddo**. They are in the **freezer**, and they don't seem to be frozen! I don't want to disappoint Lindsey on our first date! "The food is fabulous.

- 現在，問題出在冰淇淋凍糕。它們在冷凍庫裡，看起來沒有結凍的跡象！我可不想第一次約會就讓莉西失望啊！「真的很好吃。」

semifreddo 冰淇淋凍糕
freezer 冷凍庫

邊擦拭嘴角
邊讚美

- Lindsey **wipes up** her mouth and praised the food, **elegantly**. Then she dives into the semifreddo.

- 莉西邊擦拭嘴角邊讚美，看起來相當優雅。接著她開始進攻冰淇淋凍糕。

wipes up 擦掉
elegantly 優雅地

MP3 040

■ As a local, I just enjoy myself so much in teasing my **client**s about trying the **infamous** herring. Those who visit the Netherlands always have herring in mind, but very few of them really try a bite.

嘗試惡名昭彰的鯡魚

■ 做為一個當地人，我很享受捉弄我的客人們去嘗試惡名昭彰的鯡魚。來荷蘭旅遊的人都知道鯡魚，但很少有人真的願意嘗上一口。

client 客戶
infamous 惡名昭彰的

■ Since I insist, Pete finally tries a bite of the herring sandwich. Seeing his **wacky** face makes me **burst out laughing**. Oh, this guy!

咬了一口鯡魚三明治

■ 禁不起我的堅持，彼得終究咬了一口鯡魚三明治。看著他臉上微妙的表情，我捧腹大笑。唉，這個男人喔！

wacky 微妙的
burst out laughing 大笑

■ In the Netherlands, herring **peddler**s are everywhere. Due to the geographic **vantage**, herring has become one of the most known Dutch cuisines.

鯡魚小販隨處可見

■ 在荷蘭，鯡魚小販隨處可見。因著地理優勢的緣故，鯡魚儼然已成為荷蘭最出名的美食之一。

peddler 小販
vantage 優勢

■ Tina, the girl I **had a crush on** when I was 13, told me this after I asked her to be my girlfriend. I take out the potatoes, fill them with mozzarella **morsel**s and coat them with panko.

■ 我十三歲時喜歡上的女孩蒂娜，在我向她告白後這麼說。我拿出馬鈴薯泥，塞入莫札瑞拉乳酪塊，並裹上麵包粉。

have a crush on sb. 愛上某人
morsel 塊

塞入莫札瑞拉乳酪塊

■ The smell of frying these croquettes makes me happy. I **ignore** the fact that I am **abandon**ed, and I will keep fighting.

■ 油炸這些可樂餅的聲音令我快樂。我會忽略自己被拋棄的事實，並繼續奮鬥。

ignore 忽略
abandon 拋棄

油炸這些可樂餅

- Croquette is a **dish** that can be found all-over the world. The main ingredient is mashed potato; it is coated in bread **crumb**s and deep fried.

在裹上麵包粉後油炸

- 可樂餅是一項風靡全世界的美食，這道菜的主要材料是馬鈴薯泥，在裹上麵包粉後油炸。

dish 美食
crumb 碎屑

- In Asia, especially in Japan, the croquette is usually without the **filling** and served as a **street food** or a side dish.

可樂餅通常是沒有內餡的

- 在亞洲，特別是日本，可樂餅通常是沒有內餡的，常見於街頭小吃和配菜。

filling 內餡
street food 街頭小吃

澳洲牛奶濃縮咖啡、澳洲維吉麥抹醬

- Sitting in the center of Woolloomooloo, Australia, I feel **weary**. A farm owner just told me that they had no vacancy for this season. I hide myself in a coffee shop, because the sun is making me **dizzy**.

這一季他們不缺人

- 我坐在澳洲伍爾盧莫盧區的中心，感到筋疲力竭。農場主人剛告訴我，這一季他們不缺人。大太陽讓我頭暈，因此我躲到咖啡館裡。

weary 疲倦的
dizzy 頭暈目眩的

■ Whatever, just give me a **flat white**, and I will be fine for now. I **text** Johnson, a friend of mine, hoping that I can stay in his place tonight.

先給我一杯牛奶濃縮咖啡

■ 管他的，先給我一杯牛奶濃縮咖啡，至少這個當下我會覺得好過一點。我發簡訊給傑森─我的好友，並期待他今晚可以收留我。

flat white 牛奶濃縮咖啡
text 發簡訊

■ He orders a flat white too. "Now you can relax." He winks. Like the **foam thinly** laying on flat white, I like Johnson just the right amount: no more, no less.

在牛奶濃縮咖啡上那薄薄一層的奶泡

■ 他也點了一杯牛奶濃縮咖啡。「現在妳可以放鬆了。」他眨著眼說。我對傑森的感情就像躺在牛奶濃縮咖啡上那薄薄一層的奶泡，不多不少剛剛好。

foam 泡沫
thinly 薄薄一層的

■ Some claim that flat white is the Aussie name for latte, which are composed of both milk and steamed foam. However, the exact amount of milk and foam is what **distinguish**es these two.

■ 有的人宣稱牛奶濃縮咖啡只不過是拿鐵在澳洲的別名,因為這兩者都有牛奶和奶泡。然而,牛奶、奶泡用量的不同才是區分這兩者的原因。

distinguish 分辨

■ Mike generously applies a spoonful of Vegemite on toasted bread and enjoys it with a cup of black coffee. This **molasses** looking thing in front of me makes me hesitant.

■ 麥克豪邁的在烤好的吐司上抹上一大匙維吉麥抹醬,並和一杯黑咖啡一起享用。我面前這個黑糖蜜的玩意兒讓我遲疑。

molasses 黑糖蜜

■ Mike **insist**s that Vegemite is as Aussie as he is, and he "has been having it since he was a baby". I sip on my latte and **peek** at the spread.

邊偷瞄那瓶抹醬

■ 麥可堅持維吉麥抹醬跟他一樣很「澳洲」，而且他「可是從小屁孩時代吃到現在」。我邊喝拿鐵邊偷瞄那瓶抹醬。

insist 堅持
peek 偷看

■ Vegemite is a yeasty spread originated in Australia. It is considered to **be related to** British Marmite, a similar food **paste**.

發源於澳洲的酵母抹醬

■ 維吉麥抹醬是一種發源於澳洲的酵母抹醬。一般認為，它與英國馬麥抹醬（一種類似的食品糊狀製品）有關聯。

be related to 跟…有關
paste 糊；膏

紐西蘭帕洛瓦蛋糕、美國藍紋起司醬、牛排美國炭烤肋排

MP3 042

■ Yet one thing I know: she likes Pavlova. These days without seeing her, I **practice** making this cake **in the thought of** her.

喜歡帕洛瓦蛋糕

■ 然而有一件事我知道，就是她喜歡帕洛瓦蛋糕。那些見不著她的日子，我就邊想著她邊練習做這道蛋糕。

practice 練習
in the thought of 想著…

■ My heart is pounding. I can barely **breathe**, but somehow the Pavlova gets successfully into her hand. Lilia looks surprised. "I don't usually **receive** gifts from fans."

成功地將帕洛瓦蛋糕交到她的手上

■ 我的心跳得好快,幾乎快不能呼吸;然而我還是成功地將帕洛瓦蛋糕交到她的手上了。

breathe 呼吸
receive 接受

■ The steak wasn't cheap and blue cheese sounded **scary**. I was afraid that I would **waste** my money and end up wasting the steak, too.

花了錢又無福消受

■ 牛排不便宜,藍紋起司聽起來也很嚇人,我擔心到頭來會花了錢又無福消受。

scary 可怕的
waste 浪費

■ I've heard that the **sharpness** of blue cheese would **go well with** the steak, but it wasn't the thing for me. The blue cheese tasted weird.

■ 聽説藍紋起司強烈的味道跟牛排很搭，但實在不合我胃口。因為起司醬味道太怪。

sharpness 強烈
go well with 很搭

藍紋起司強烈的味道跟牛排很搭

■ Meat, in any case, is essential to human race, not to mention the golden brown, crispy yet **juicy** ribs. When they are coated in barbecue sauce, what else in the world can **compete with** it?

■ 再怎麼説，肉對人類而言都是必需品，更別説是金黃酥脆、鮮嫩多汁的炭烤肋排。當肋排裹上 BBQ 醬汁，世間還有什麼能與之匹敵呢？

juicy 多汁的
compete with 與之競爭

金黃酥脆、鮮嫩多汁的炭烤肋排

當肉在烤架上滋滋作響

- The ribs **that are done right** are the most amazing food in the world. The **sizzling** sound while cooking on a grill, and the smell slowly coming out is going to take you to another world.

- 料理得恰到好處,肋排是世界上最美味的食物。當肉在烤架上滋滋作響,那漸漸烤熟的香氣可是會把你帶到另一個世界。

  that are done right 恰到好處
  sizzling 滋滋的

肋排價位較高

- Ribs are rather **expensive** comparing to other kind of meat, so I don't **regret** that I am not a fan of it.

- 跟其他部位的肉相比,肋排價位較高,所以我不會因為自己不為肋排瘋狂而感到遺憾。

  expensive 昂貴的
  regret 遺憾

Unit 43　炸魚條、美國加州捲、美國雞肉深鍋派

MP3 043

■ White fish can hardly be compared with tuna or **salmon**. They don't possess so much flavor **naturally**. The fish is bland, but with bread crumbs and a little bit of ketchup – yum!

> 裏上麵包粉，抹上番茄醬之後

■ 白身魚很難跟鮪魚或鮭魚相比；它們生來就沒那麼有滋味。魚本身雖滋味平淡，但裏上麵包粉，抹上番茄醬之後，哇，真好吃！

salmon 鮭魚
naturally 自然地

■ Delicacies, fish sticks can't even be considered **cuisine**. Yet talking about the flavor itself, these breaded sticks can easily get you hooked. They taste clean, sort of simple but **delicious**.

炸魚條倒扯不上邊

■ 我在美味方面是絕對同意的。至於說這是精緻美饌，炸魚條倒扯不上邊。單純談味道面的話，這些裹了粉的魚柳真的很容易讓人上癮。

cuisine 佳餚
delicious 美味的

■ **California roll** is super great. They are not like sushi, which is always dull and goes by the book. I don't care if people call it a bad **imitation**.

糟糕的仿造品

■ 加州捲超讚。它們不像壽司往往是乏味、照本宣科做出來的。我常不按牌理出牌，而加州捲就是這樣的料理。我才不在乎有人說它是糟糕的仿造品。

California roll 加州捲
imitation 仿造品

1 生活、娛樂、科技和交通

2 異國飲食和人文風情

3 教育、知識、學習

4 工作和金錢的使用

■ California roll, however, **triumph**s on appearance and on taste. It is more colorful and more complex. I especially like **avocado** and fried banana; it's less expensive yet so satisfying!

特別喜歡酪梨和炸香蕉的組合

■ 加州捲在外表和味道上都勝出，其顏色豐富且多樣。我特別喜歡酪梨和炸香蕉的組合，既經濟又實惠！

triumph 勝過
avocado 酪梨

■ The California roll, on the other hand, can have so many **combination**s! For me, I'd rather pay the same amount of money and have **simple** but concentrated food.

味道由鹹到甜都有

■ 加州捲呢，則有相當多組合；價錢由高至低、味道由鹹到甜都有。對我來說，我偏好付同樣的價錢，選擇簡單但純粹的壽司。

combination 組合
simple 簡單的

■ There are potatoes, carrots, **pea**s, and chicken, all in the meaty- creamy **gravy**. I especially appreciate the crust on top; it gives more body to the whole dish.

浸潤在肉味香濃又濃郁的奶汁裡

■ 派裡有馬鈴薯、胡蘿蔔、豌豆仁和雞肉，全浸潤在肉味香濃又濃郁的奶汁裡。我特別喜歡上頭那層派皮，它讓整道菜更完整。

pea 豌豆
gravy 肉汁（作調味用的）滷

■ Chicken pot pie is such a **hearty** dish for me that I can literary eat it every day! The creaminess **comforts** not only the stomach, but also the heart.

是道暖心料理

■ 雞肉深鍋派是道暖心料理，我可以每天吃！雞肉派不僅餵飽了肚腹，更滿足了心靈。

hearty 暖心的
comfort 撫慰

MP3 044

■ I visited Dominique Ansel's bakery in New York, of course, and got the real deal. Although the fake ones are everywhere, it is not **comparable** to the real thing! Here is my cronut experience: **crispy**, delicate, and beautiful.

享用真正道地
的可拿滋

■ 我造訪了位在紐約的多明尼克・安西烘焙坊，並享用真正道地的可拿滋。雖然仿冒的可拿滋隨處可得，但那跟真貨可沒得比。如果你想要好味道，可得尋本溯源，對吧？我的可拿滋經驗如下：酥脆、精緻、美麗。

comparable 可比較的
crispy 酥脆的

去 Mister Donut 買可拿滋

■ I had my cronuts in Mister Donut, and they are pretty decent. The only fault is that sometimes the dough can be tricky and become **greasy**. It depends on the chef and on luck, I guess.

■ 我都是去 Mister Donut 買可拿滋，他們做得不錯。唯一的缺點是，有時候麵糊不易掌控，結果弄得油膩膩。這要看糕餅師的技術和運氣了，我想。

greasy 油膩膩的

等於麥當勞一個漢堡

■ A cupcake can **go up to** $4 and that's like a burger in McDonald's. Instead of fancy yet **sugary** cakes, I'd rather go for savory sandwiches.

■ 一個杯子蛋糕可達售價四美元，等於麥當勞一個漢堡。要我吃個漂亮但膩人的蛋糕，我寧願選正餐三明治。

go up to 可達
sugary 膩人的

■ Having cupcakes in Magnolia Bakery is a **must-do** in New York, not only because it's featured in *Sex and the City*, but also because the flavor that makes it a **spectacular** taste.

■ 造訪紐約一定不可錯過蒙哥利亞烘焙坊，不僅是因其出現在《慾望城市》裡，更因那無與倫比的好味道。

無與倫比的好味道

must-do 必做的
spectacular 無與倫比的

■ I had frog legs hot pot in Jakarta, Indonesia. The legs were cooked with vegetables until tender, served with rice and some **pickle**s. I love the **combination** of soup and rice.

■ 我曾在印尼雅加達吃到蛙腿火鍋；蛙腿和蔬菜一起燉煮到柔軟，搭配白飯和醃菜。我喜歡有湯有飯的感覺。

喜歡有湯有飯的感覺

pickle 醃菜
combination 組合

油炸蛙腿多
汁、酥脆

■ I've only eaten one kind of frog legs: deep-fried. The breading process completely covers up the shape, which makes it more **appetizing**. Deep-fried frog legs are juicy, crunchy, and they **go perfectly with** sweet-spicy sauce.

■ 我只吃一種蛙腿料理：油炸蛙腿。因為裹了粉的緣故，完全看不出蛙腿的形狀，感覺比較吃得下去。油炸蛙腿多汁、酥脆，跟甜辣沾醬很搭。

appetizing 開胃的
go perfectly with 很搭

喜歡用檸檬汁
和西洋芹料理
的蛙腿

■ I like the fact that they cook frog legs with lemon juice and parsley. It eliminates the disgusting earthy flavor that I expect to have, and the plate adds color to the dish.

■ 我喜歡用檸檬汁和西洋芹料理的蛙腿，不僅沒有我預期的噁心土味，餐盤看起來顏色漂亮。

MP3 045

■ I have to say that comparing to French **escargot**s, I prefer Asian grilled snails. I like that the **fishermen** just catch the snail at the coast and grill them on the spot.

偏好亞洲風燒烤螺肉

■ 我必須説比起法式蝸牛，我偏好亞洲風燒烤螺肉。我喜歡漁夫們在海邊抓螺，並當場燒烤。

escargot 食用蝸牛
fishermen 漁夫們

- The sea snails are infused by **red pepper**, rice wine and a hint of **saltiness** from the sea. Asian food has bold flavor, and watching men moving their hands to catch and cook those fruits of the sea is such a pleasure.

亞洲料理都有鮮明的味道

- 這些海螺加入紅辣椒、米酒和大海的鹹味一起料理。亞洲料理都有鮮明的味道，而看著人們舞動抓螺、料理實在是種饗宴。

red pepper 紅辣椒
saltiness 鹹味

- French escargots are stuffed with **pesto** and sprinkled with cheese. It kind of turns these creepy-looking **Mollusk**s into another delicacy.

塞了青醬並撒上起司

- 法式蝸牛塞了青醬並撒上起司，幾乎讓這些令人起雞皮疙瘩的軟體動物變成一道佳餚了。

pesto 青醬
mollusk 軟體動物

■ It's such a **classic** food that none should miss out on. My **ideal** chicken roulade must have sun-dried tomatoes, spinach and prosciutto. I like it clean, simple, and rich.

■ 我心目中的雞肉捲必須包含油漬番茄乾、菠菜和帕瑪火腿。我喜歡乾淨、簡單和豐盛的感覺。

classic 經典的
ideal 理想的

■ All the flavors will **add up** when there is prosciutto. A perfect chicken roulade needs to have a perfect **crust** and a juicy interior.

■ 只要有帕瑪火腿,所有味道都會獲得提升。一道完美的雞肉捲需要有漂亮的焦脆外層,以及多汁的肉。

add up 提升
crust 外層

■ I've heard that **jellied eel** can be dated back to the 18th century, when people were starving most of the time. Someone then started to catch eels from the River Thames and cook them with **limited** ingredients.

從泰晤士河中抓取鰻魚

■ 我聽說鰻魚凍是在十八世紀時，因為人們常處在飢餓的狀態之中，有人便開始從泰晤士河中抓取鰻魚，並與有限的材料一起烹煮。

jellied eel 鰻魚凍
limited 有限的

■ The **result** is the jellied eel we have today. I feel sad eating this dish, because eel is so **delicious** in other countries like Japan!

在日本可是佳餚啊

■ 其結果便是我們今天看到的鰻魚凍。吃這道菜讓我覺得難過，因為鰻魚在日本可是佳餚啊！

result 成果
delicious 美味的

1 生活、娛樂、科技和交通

2 異國飲食和人文風情

3 教育、知識、學習

4 工作和金錢的使用

愛爾蘭鹽醃牛肉、義大利玉米粥、義大利焗烤千層茄

MP3 046

■ Corned beef by itself is not my favorite. I think it's **reasonable** that I go for fresh steak, right? However, I do love corned beef hash. After St. Patrick's day, there are usually **leftovers**.

喜歡炒醃牛肉碎

■ 純粹的鹽醃牛肉我不愛。我覺得棄之而取新鮮牛排可以理解,對吧?不過,我的確很喜歡炒醃牛肉碎。在聖派翠克節過後,通常都有剩菜。

reasonable 合理的
leftover 剩菜

■ Corned beef with **turnip**s, potatoes and carrots really creates a **balanced** hash. It's even better than a hash brown, I have to admit. I am certainly a big fan of that.

（比炸薯餅還好吃）

■ 鹽醃牛肉和蕪菁、馬鈴薯及胡蘿蔔共同譜出和諧的樂章。我必須承認，這幾乎比炸薯餅還好吃！我真的超愛。

turnip 蕪菁
balanced 和諧的

■ **Polenta** is not on my list of delicacies. Polenta reminds me of English porridge, and that is the food served in an **orphanage**. That is one of the last foods that I would eat.

（聯想到英式燕麥粥）

■ 玉米粥不在我的美食清單上。玉米粥讓我聯想到英式燕麥粥，那是孤兒院的伙食欸。這是我最不想吃的食物之一。

polenta 玉米粥
orphanage 孤兒院

偏好固態的玉米粥

■ I prefer solid polenta over a wet one. When it's made with less water, it becomes more like a loaf than a bowl of porridge. It's easier to slice, grill and become a **condiment** on the plate.

■ 我偏好固態的玉米粥，不喜歡液狀的。如果烹調時使用較少的水，玉米粥就會形成條狀，而非粥狀。這樣就比較容易切片、烘烤，成為美味的佐料。

condiment 佐料

玉米粥充滿奶香

■ It's so creamy and vibrant, and a sprinkle of herbs really brightens it up. Polenta also becomes a necessity when it comes to **ragout**, which is quite frequently used in Italian and European cuisine.

■ 這樣的玉米粥充滿奶香，令人振奮，幾撮香草更是畫龍點睛。若提到義大利及歐陸菜餚中常出現的燉肉，玉米粥更是不可或缺的存在。

ragout 蔬菜燉肉

焗烤千層茄看
起來很油膩

■ Somehow, Italian foods all have this common point: cheese, baked, and **marinara** sauce. The thing about eggplant parmesan is that it looks heavy, but actually it melts in your mouth.

■ 怎麼說呢，義大利菜有些共通點，那就是起司、烘烤、和番茄紅醬。焗烤千層茄看起來很油膩，但其實入口即化。

marinara 大蒜番茄醬

混合了義大利
香料和帕瑪善
起司的麵包粉

■ Moreover, although the marinara sauce covers the whole thing, it's not overpowering. The secret might be the breading on the eggplant, which is a **mixture** of bread crumbs, Italian spices and parmesan cheese.

■ 還有，雖然番茄紅醬淹過整道菜，卻不會只嘗到番茄味。其秘訣或許是裹在茄子上那層混合了義大利香料和帕瑪善起司的麵包粉。

mixture 混合

義大利餃、德國豬腳、波蘭餃

 MP3 047

■ I feel like the ravioli are another kind of pizza; you can put anything in there, and you can apply any kind of sauce on them. I especially like deep-fried **ravioli**. It's like a **wonton** with a tastier skin.

填料可以自由發揮

■ 義大利餃給我的感覺是另類披薩，因為填料可以自由發揮，醬汁也可以任意選擇。我特別喜愛油炸義大利餃，感覺像有著美味外皮的餛飩。

ravioli 義大利餃
wonton 餛飩

■ Unlike **linguine**, ravioli don't get you messy. As for the filling, I'm not someone innovative. Red sauce and **ground beef** would be my choice.

> 紅醬和牛絞肉就是我的最愛了

■ 不像細麵，義大利餃不會搞得你髒兮兮。至於內餡，我是沒什麼新點子啦，紅醬和牛絞肉就是我的最愛了。

linguine 細麵
ground beef 牛絞肉

■ **Roasted** Schweinshaxe, on the other hand, is juicy and **pulls apart**. It goes so well with German beers, so if you are a fan, this is your choice.

> 一碰即骨肉分離

■ 相較於此，燒烤的豬腳多汁又柔軟，一碰即骨肉分離。豬腳跟德國啤酒很搭，如果你是好此道者，選這道菜準沒錯。

roasted 燒烤的
pull apart 分離

酸味中和了肉味

■ Normally, I don't enjoy a big chunk of meat, but I do feel more comfortable to eat it along with **sauerkraut**. I believe that the acid kills the meaty taste and makes it more enjoyable.

■ 通常我是不吃這麼大塊肉的,但跟德國酸菜一起吃就沒問題。我想酸味中和了肉味,讓這道菜更可口。

sauerkraut 一種德國泡菜

油炸會產生另類口感,也就是酥脆感

■ Roasting is one good way to cook this big piece of delicacy, but deep-frying creates another **texture** which is **crispy**. I like them both, and a bottle of Schwarzbier, German black beer, will complete this meal.

■ 燒烤是料理這一塊大肉的好方法,但是油炸會產生另類口感,也就是酥脆感。我兩種都喜歡,特別要搭上一瓶德國黑啤酒,整頓飯就圓滿了。

texture 口感
crispy 酥脆的

■ The filling is composed of mashed potatoes and cottage cheese, and the **dumplings** are **garnish**ed with fried onions. I wish there was a sauce to dip in.

餃子上以炸洋蔥裝飾

■ 其內餡以馬鈴薯泥和農舍起司製成，餃子上以炸洋蔥裝飾。這組合不會太詭異，但滋味平淡。我希望至少有醬汁可以沾。

dumpling 水餃
garnish 添加配菜於

■ Pierogi is a delicious dish to me. It **reflects** the **diet** of Polish people, which I think it's very cool. Unlike the French, Italian or Chinese, Polish eating is all about "not being hungry."

波蘭式飲食全在於「吃飽」

■ 波蘭餃對我來說是很好吃的一道菜，它反映了波蘭人的飲食，我認為很酷。不像法式、義式或中式，波蘭式飲食全在於「吃飽」。

reflect 反映
diet 飲食

MP3 048

■ My personal **preference** for fondue base is two kinds of cheese, unsweetened white wine and garlic paste. As for the dipping, nothing compares to two tips of **medium rare** filet mignon. Cheese, beef and wine.

> 兩種起士、不甜白酒和蒜泥

■ 我個人偏好的起士鍋底是兩種起士、不甜白酒和蒜泥。至於沾料，沒什麼比得上三分熟的菲力骰子牛。起司、牛排和酒。

preference 偏好
medium rare 三分熟

■ It's said that cheese fondue was invented by **lumberjacks** in the mountains. Due to the cold weather and the energy-consuming labor, they need fondue as their calorie supply. Whether it's true or not, cheese fondue is definitely a rich dish.

起士鍋作為熱量補給來源

■ 據說起士鍋是伐木工在山上發明的。因著天氣嚴寒及勞力需求的工作，他們需要起士鍋作為熱量補給來源。不論真相如何，起士鍋絕對是道濃郁的料理。

lumberjacks 伐木工

■ It's **crucial**, though, that Yorkshire pudding is properly prepared and baked. If it loses its **crispiness**, it's nothing more than a soggy mess.

布丁失去脆度

■ 不過，確實的準備並烘烤約克夏布丁很關鍵。如果布丁失去脆度，就會淪為一團軟爛的漿糊。

crucial 關鍵的
crispiness 脆度

1 生活、娛樂、科技和交通

2 異國飲食和人文風情

3 教育、知識、學習

4 工作和金錢的使用

■ I adore an alluring **freshly-baked** Yorkshire pudding. It's screaming for whipped cream and honey. And that's what I always do – dump the **sweet elements** in there and dig right in.

■ 我還是很喜歡剛出爐的約克夏布丁；那布丁幾乎是尖叫著要打發鮮奶油和蜂蜜！而我當然照辦－把甜蜜的元素淋上布丁，然後開動！

freshly-baked 出爐的
sweet element 甜蜜的元素

喜歡剛出爐的約克夏布丁

■ It has been a long time since I had a **kebab**. It's certainly not an elegant food. It has nothing to do with **fine dining**.

■ 我上次吃串烤是很久以前了。這絕對不是高貴的食物，跟精緻美食扯不上邊。

kebab 串烤
fine dining 精緻美食

跟精緻美食扯不上邊

- Being able to hunt and to cook with fire are two of human's basic **survival needs**. I believe that's why kebabs are always **appealing** to people no matter where they are.

最原始的兩項
生存技能

- 打獵和烤肉是人類最原始的兩項生存需求，我想這就是無論在哪裡，串烤總是引人食慾的原因。

survival needs 生存需求
appealing 吸引人的

- My favorite kebab skewer comprises of garlic, bell pepper, **zucchini**, and tomato. When the vegetables are **charred**, they become very tender and extremely juicy.

非常柔軟
且多汁

- 我最愛的串烤食材有大蒜、甜椒、櫛瓜和番茄。蔬菜燒烤之後，會變得非常柔軟且多汁。

zucchini 櫛瓜
charred 燒烤的

1
生活、娛樂、科技和交通

2
異國飲食和人文風情

3
教育、知識、學習

4
工作和金錢的使用

211

MP3 049

■ It was quite a challenge for me to try **Baklava**. I think the desserts from Turkey and the Mediterranean area are overly sweet, and I've **sworn off** them ever since I tried Turkish delights.

太過甜膩了

■ 吃果仁蜜餅對我來説是個挑戰。我覺得土耳其和地中海一帶的點心都太過甜膩了，自從我吃了土耳其軟糖之後，我就對這些甜點敬而遠之。

Baklava 果仁蜜餅
sworn off 敬而遠之

■ I have had Baklava many times. The crucial element of a good Baklava is the **honey**. Honey is the soul of this dessert.

■ 我吃過果仁蜜餅很多次了，要做出好的果仁蜜餅，重點是蜂蜜。蜂蜜是這道甜點的靈魂。

honey 蜂蜜

蜂蜜是這道甜點的靈魂

■ **Savory**, sweet, whatever, I just love the **fluffiness** of the eggy toast. My NO.1 French toast is at Sarabeth's in New York. Their secret of making such soft and juicy French toast remains hidden.

■ 正餐或甜點都沒差，我就是愛那鬆鬆軟軟的蛋香味。紐約莎拉貝斯的法式吐司是我心目中的第一名，他們做出極致鬆軟多汁法式吐司的秘訣仍然成謎。

極致鬆軟多汁

savory 正餐
fluffiness 鬆鬆軟軟

1 生活、娛樂、科技和交通

2 異國飲食和人文風情

3 教育、知識、學習

4 工作和金錢的使用

■ I was first exposed to **French toast** in Tokyo. The French toast was surrounded with fresh berries, accompanied by a mountain of whipped cream. Watching those tiny Japanese girls crying "kawaii" was an interesting thing.

■ 我第一次吃法式吐司是在東京，吐司四周放著新鮮莓果，還有像小山一般的打發鮮奶油。看著那些嬌小的日本女孩尖叫著「好可愛！」是挺新奇的體驗，

French toast 法式吐司

四周放著新鮮莓果

■ I am a supporter of French toast. I think it's a beautiful and satisfying brunch for ladies when we want to have some **indulgence**. My favorite combination is fruit with syrup, and that's it.

■ 我是法式吐司愛好者，我覺得這是當女性想要稍微放縱時，一道美觀又令人滿足的早午餐。我最愛的組合是水果和糖漿，就這樣而已。

indulgence 放縱

美觀又令人滿足的早午餐

■ I associate it with American candies that have this gummy texture, and **artificial** flavor. It's kind of fake but salty at the same time. Personally, I don't hate Salmiakki.

吃起來又假又鹹

■ 我覺得那跟美國那些充滿人工香精味的軟糖滿像的，吃起來又假又鹹。我個人沒那麼討厭甘草糖

artificial 人工的

■ I have tasted different forms of Salmiakki: Salmiakki-flavored soda candy, soft candy, **sugar-coated** versions, etc. I think the saltiness and the chemicals in there have an effect like **caffeine**.

有種類似咖啡因的效果

■ 我吃過許多不同形式的甘草糖，比如甘草糖口味的汽水糖、軟糖、裹了砂糖的口味等等。我覺得甘草糖的鹹味和它的成份有種類似咖啡因的效果

sugar-coated 裹了砂糖的
caffeine 咖啡因

葡式蛋塔、西班牙牛軋糖、法國可麗餅

■ It's not like a typical pastry that only has a soft part; there is a hard shell protecting its **gooey** center. The main **attraction** of Pastel de Nata is the contrast between crunchy and soft, solid and fluid.

> 葡式蛋塔軟糊的內餡外包著硬脆的塔皮

■ 不像一般甜點只有柔軟的口感,葡式蛋塔軟糊的內餡外包著硬脆的塔皮。它吸引人的主要原因,就是酥脆和柔軟、堅硬和軟糯的衝突感。

gooey 膠黏的
attraction 吸引力

216

■ In Macao, China, people line up for freshly-baked Pastel de Natas. The size is a bit bigger than the **original** one, but I like the fact that it's less **sugary**.

剛出爐的葡式蛋塔

■ 在中國澳門，人們排著長長的隊伍要買剛出爐的葡式蛋塔。這兒的尺寸稍大一些，但比較不甜，我喜歡。

original 原本的
sugary 甜的

■ Just like churro is a victory for Spain, Pastel de Nata is a glory of **Portugal**. I was amazed by the golden crust and the shiny custard filling when I first saw a Pastel de Nata.

葡式蛋塔也是葡萄牙的榮耀

■ 就像吉拿棒是西班牙的勝利一樣，葡式蛋塔也是葡萄牙的榮耀。我第一次看到葡式蛋塔時，為其金黃色的塔皮及閃耀的卡士達內餡所震懾。

Portugal 葡萄牙

蛋白需臻
至完美

■ In order to achieve the best texture, **egg whites** play a crucial role. They need to be perfectly incorporated, so the **nougat** won't become too hard or too chewy.

■ 為了維持最好的口感,蛋白相當重要。蛋白需臻至完美,牛軋糖才不致太硬或太彈牙。

egg whites 蛋白
nougat 牛軋糖

使用蛋白來做
為黏合的材料

■ Nougat is a candy bar that combines dried fruit and nuts. Egg whites are used as a **binder** for the texture. Usually, I only have nougat on **festival**s or holidays, such as Christmas.

■ 軋糖是由水果乾和堅果組成的糖果棒,並使用蛋白來做為黏合的材料。通常我只在節慶日子享用牛軋糖,比如說耶誕節。

binder 黏合
festival 節慶

■ I will say that the crêpe suzette is pretty **fancy** – especially when it is on fire. It is a table trick that can **catch customers' eyes** and make them come back.

> 火焰可麗餅的確很吸睛

■ 我承認火焰可麗餅的確很吸睛,特別是著火的那幾秒。那是種桌邊秀,可以讓客人感到驚豔進而吸引顧客回流。

fancy 豪華的
catch customers' eyes 吸引顧客目光

■ It is impossible. The soft and **fluffy** texture filled with fruit, chocolate and whipped cream is **heaven** in the mouth. I've also tried savory crêpes.

> 在嘴裡綻放的滋味簡直像天堂

■ 軟綿綿的餅皮配上水果、巧克力醬和打發鮮奶油,在嘴裡綻放的滋味簡直像天堂!我也有吃過鹹的可麗餅

fluffy 軟綿綿的
heaven 天堂

法國烤布蕾、法國馬卡龍、印度南餅

 MP3 051

- I love to have crème brûlée as a happy ending to my dining experience. In Asia, however, crème brûlée seems to be really easy to get, but the **quality** is **questionable**.

烤布蕾似乎非常容易取得

- 我喜歡以烤布蕾作為美好晚餐的句點。然而，在亞洲，烤布蕾似乎非常容易取得，品質卻沒有保證。

quality 品質
questionable 受質疑的

■ Custard applied with some cream doesn't equal a crème brûlée. In my book, it has to have this perfect **layer** of **caramelization** on top, as crispy as a piece of glass almost.

> 烤布蕾必須有上面那層完美的焦糖

■ 卡士達加上一些奶油不等於烤布蕾。依我來看，烤布蕾必須有上面那層完美的焦糖，幾乎像玻璃般易碎才行。

layer 層
caramelization 焦糖

■ The French are famous for their passion for dessert, and a dessert means there is sugar. Hence, a bowl of **well-sweetened** custard really **scares me away**.

> 甜點等於砂糖

■ 法國人對甜點是有名的著迷，而甜點等於砂糖，因此一碗紮紮實實、甜蜜蜜的卡士達真的會把我嚇跑。

well-sweetened 紮紮實實、甜蜜蜜的
scare me away 把我嚇跑

221

■ I like dessert, **don't get me wrong**. Nevertheless, a macaron is basically powdered sugar and **almond flour**, and flavoring. It may please your eyes, but it's certainly not exciting to eat.

■ 不要誤會喔，我喜歡吃甜點。但是，馬卡龍基本上就是糖粉、杏仁粉和調味。視覺上可能很吸睛，但吃起來沒什麼刺激感。

don't get me wrong 不要誤會喔
almond flour 杏仁粉

馬卡龍基本上就是糖粉、杏仁粉和調味

■ Macaron is a fancy thing for me. It is moist, sugary and cute. I admit that **it's got a reason to be famous**, but it is not that **appealing** to me.

■ 馬卡龍對我來說是個酷炫的玩意兒。它濕潤、甜蜜又可愛。我承認它有爆紅是有原因的，但是對我而言沒太大吸引力。

it's got a reason to be famous 它有爆紅的理由
appealing 吸引人的

是個酷炫的玩意

■ The first time I tried naan bread was as a flatbread pizza. I like the crunchy edges and the **elastic** interior. What I like is to pull naan bread apart and dip it in butter chicken. Simple, but heavenly.

把南餅撕成
小片沾印度
奶油雞來吃

■ 我第一次吃南餅是當披薩品嘗，我很喜歡邊邊酥脆的部分和有彈性的內裡。我喜歡把南餅撕成小片沾印度奶油雞來吃。

elastic 有彈性的

■ Among all, I love butter naan the most. When it comes out of the oven, melted butter is quickly applied on the bread, creating a **shiny golden** color and buttery smell.

出爐立刻抹上
融化的奶油

■ 在所有口味之中，我最愛奶油南餅。南餅一出爐立刻抹上融化的奶油，這會在表面形成閃耀的金黃色和奶香味。

shiny 閃耀的
golden 金黃色的

223

MP3 052

■ The only thing I can possibly accept is salmon oyako don. If I pour **sauce** over the whole thing, I don't seem to taste the **raw fish** flavor, and that's what I want.

吃不出生魚肉的味道

■ 唯一我可能可以接受的是鮭魚親子丼,如果我把醬汁淋在整碗丼飯上,我就吃不出生魚肉的味道了,那正是我要的。

sauce 醬汁
raw fish 生魚肉

■ I **selectively** like sashimi. Salmon, tuna, shrimp are the basic items. I don't like **octopus**; it is one of the weirdest seafood to eat raw. Sashimi recalls me of tartare.

■ 我選擇性地喜歡生魚片。鮭魚、鮪魚和蝦子是基本品項。我不喜歡章魚，那是最怪異的生食海鮮之一。生魚片讓我想到韃靼料理。

鮭魚、鮪魚和蝦子是基本品項

selectively 選擇性地
octopus 章魚

■ Natt　is something hard to be crazy about; actually, it is **notorious**. Although it has high **nutrient** value, for most of us, it's still hard to embrace.

■ 納豆很難討人喜歡，事實上，它臭名遠播。雖然納豆營養價值高，對大多數人而言還是難以接受。

納豆營養價值高

notorious 臭名遠播的
nutrient 營養素

- I've found two different ways to enjoy this sticky devil. The first way is to add **soy sauce** to it, mix in **raw egg** and pour on rice. The second way is to put natt   in a curry.

- 我找到兩種享受這種黏糊糊的食物的方法，一是加入醬油和生蛋並倒在飯上，二是把納豆加入咖哩中。

兩種享受這種黏糊糊的食物的方法

soy sauce 醬油
raw egg 生蛋

- The aroma of pork, garlic and **shallots** burst out, creating a "delicious" **signal** in my brain. In a few seconds, I found myself having emptied the bowl and wanting for more.

- 豬肉、大蒜和紅蔥頭的香氣併發，在腦中產生美味的訊號。數秒之後，我發現自己將碗中飧一掃而空，還想再來一碗！

在腦中產生美味的訊號

shallot 紅蔥頭
signal 訊號

喜歡飯上那片
黃色的醃蘿蔔

■ I enjoy eating on a street **vendor** seat and being surrounded by local people. I especially like the yellowish pickled daikon on the rice; it reminds me of **rustic** farmer food.

■ 我很享受在路邊攤被當地人圍繞著吃飯。我特別喜歡飯上那片黃色的醃蘿蔔，很有樸實農夫菜的風格。

vendor 攤販
rustic 樸實的

油脂會
提升味道

■ The Chinese believe that some fat helps **elevate** the flavor; thus, after a long time simmering on a stove, the result is a pot of **sticky** and fragrant pork stew.

■ 中國人相信油脂會提升味道，因此長時間在爐上燉煮之後，結果是一鍋黏稠且芬芳的滷肉。

elevate 提升
sticky 黏稠的

1 生活、娛樂、科技和交通

2 異國飲食和人文風情

3 教育、知識、學習

4 工作和金錢的使用

馬來西亞肉骨茶、韓國人參雞湯、中國左宗棠雞

 MP3 053

- I'm not crazy about bak kut the because it's not visually appealing, but I do get the **unique** flavor profile of this dish. The tender ribs are **flavorful** and go well with hot sauce.

柔軟的肋排很有滋味

- 我是沒有很喜歡肉骨茶啦,因為看起來不特別好吃,但我的確感受到這道菜獨特的個性。柔軟的肋排很有滋味,沾點辣醬很對味。

unique 獨特的
flavorful 有滋味的

- Thanks to a **time-consuming** cooking process, the pork releases its flavor into the broth and actually gives some **depth** to it.

給了湯頭深度

- 長時間的熬煮過程，豬肉的滋味被完全釋放到湯裡，這給了湯頭深度。

time-consuming 耗時的
depth 深度

- I'm a big fan of bak kut the. I think it's smart to **char** the ribs and cook them in Chinese **spice-infused** broth. For me, it's a success.

加了中國香料的高湯裡煮

- 我很喜歡肉骨茶。將煎過的豬肋排放在加了中國香料的高湯裡煮，我覺得很妙。對我來說，這道菜很成功。

char 煎
spice-infused 充滿香料的

■ Samgyetang is a dish that combines soup, rice and meat all in one pot. I couldn't have more respect and **gratitude** for the creator of this recipe.

對這道菜的發明者充滿尊敬和感謝

■ 人參雞湯是一道結合了湯、飯和肉的料理，我對這道菜的發明者充滿尊敬和感謝。雞肉裡塞滿了米飯和香料，幾乎是入口即化。

gratitude 感謝

■ Samgyetang is not just about the chicken and the rice. It is more about the **kimchi** and pickled veggies that come along with it. In Korea, kimchi and **pickled veggies** are daily necessities.

泡菜和醃漬菜是每日必需品

■ 人參雞湯不只有雞肉和米飯，還包含泡菜及其他隨之上桌的小菜。在韓國，泡菜和醃漬菜是每日必需品。

kimchi 泡菜
pickled veggies 醃漬菜

■ General Tso's chicken meets every factor I know about Chinese food. It's **greasy**, heavy-handed, and oily. It's not like Italian dishes, which are creamy, or French dishes, which are **delicate**.

不像奶香濃郁的義大利菜

■ 左宗棠雞符合每項我印象中的中國菜會有的特徵：油膩膩又重鹹。不像奶香濃郁的義大利菜，也不像精緻的法是料理。

greasy 油膩的
delicate 精緻的

■ I'm in love with General Tso's chicken. Yes, it's greasy and heavy, but it's also **addictive**! The balance of sweetness and savory points is spot-on, and the chicken is just cooked to perfection.

甜鹹平衡的感覺很棒

■ 我超喜歡左宗棠雞！沒錯，的確又油又重鹹，但同時也很讓人上癮！甜鹹平衡的感覺很棒，雞肉也煮得恰到好處。

addictive 上癮的

MP3 054

- The way it is served — **shredded** ginger and a little bit of soy sauce and vinegar, is probably the secret to making it tastier. Although it looks kind of **bland**, somehow you just can't help but eat one after another.

這些包子外表並不起眼

- 薑絲、幾滴醬油和醋大概是讓小籠包更美味的秘密。雖然這些包子外表並不起眼，但就是會無法控制的一個接一個吃下去。簡直像著魔一樣呢！

shredded 碎的
bland 平淡無奇的

■ Din Tai Fung has taken this civilian dish to another level. It is delicate, specific, and well-designed. Whoever has been there can testify that the astonishment of the gravy bursts in your mouth is an **indescribable** experience.

精緻、規格嚴謹、設計獨到

■ 鼎泰豐卻把這種平民小吃帶入另一個層次。這些包子精緻、規格嚴謹、設計獨到。只要是去過的人都可以見證，肉汁在你嘴裡爆開時的驚喜，是絕非筆墨所能形容。

indescribable 非筆墨所能形容的

■ In Bangkok, there are so many Pad Thai peddlers, but very few of them serve bad food. Classic flavor: shrimp with fish sauce, bean sprout and chili is my favorite.

炒河粉的攤販很多

■ 在曼谷，炒河粉的攤販很多，但僅有少數會供應難吃的食物。經典口味：蝦子配魚露、豆芽菜和辣椒是我的最愛。

1 生活、娛樂、科技和交通

2 異國飲食和人文風情

3 教育、知識、學習

4 工作和金錢的使用

■ I prefer **sitting in the open air**. There, I am more at ease. Also, I don't only enjoy the food, but seeing the people. It's very **exotic**.

■ 偏好坐在露天座

■ 我偏好坐在露天座，感覺很自在。在享受食物的同時，我還能看看路邊的人。這是相當異國風情的體驗。

sitting in the open air 坐在露天座
exotic 異國風情的

■ I like the crushed peanuts on Pad Thai. It's not crunchy, but it's **aromatic**. Also, I love the rice noodles. The **chewiness** is found nowhere else.

嚼勁的口感別處可找不到

■ 我喜歡泰式炒河粉上面的花生碎，吃起來不會卡滋卡滋的，但是很香。還有，我好愛河粉喔。那有嚼勁的口感別處可找不到啊。

aromatic 芳香的
chewiness 嚼勁

■ Basically, dango is made of **sticky rice powder** and water. Then it's boiled and coated with **condiments** such as Anzuki bean paste, flavored sugar or sauce.

用糯米粉和水製成

■ 基本上，糰子是用糯米粉和水製成，之後水煮並裹上紅豆泥、調味砂糖或醬汁。

sticky rice powder 糯米粉
condiment 佐料

■ Dango is usually served on a **bamboo skewer**, and that makes it easy and **elegant** to eat. I like soy sauce soaked dango.

方便吃，又能吃得優雅

■ 糰子通常以竹籤串成，這樣既方便吃，又能吃得優雅。我喜歡醬油糰子。

bamboo skewer 竹籤串
elegant 優雅的

1
生活、娛樂、科技和交通

2
異國飲食和人文風情

3
教育、知識、學習

4
工作和金錢的使用

235

MP3 055

■ The traditional one is made of Chinese **hawthorn**, but nowadays the variations are fancier. I like **stuffed tomato preserves**; they are savory and sweet.

■ 傳統糖葫蘆使用仙楂，但今天各種水果都有。我喜歡蜜餞番茄，嘗起來甜甜鹹鹹的。

hawthorn 仙楂
stuffed tomato preserves 蜜餞番茄

傳統糖葫蘆使用仙楂

■ Tanghulu used to be sold only in winter, but now they are sold all-year round. They are at their best in winter, though, because the **heat** will **melt** down their crispy sugar coat.

■ 糖葫蘆以前只在冬天販售，但現在四季都找得到。我想還是冬天買最好，因為暑氣會把糖葫蘆外層的結晶糖融化掉。

heat 熱
melt 融化

> 暑氣會把糖葫蘆外層的結晶糖融化掉

■ Tanhulu reminds me of candy apples. The **vivid** color and the **sweetness** seemed to enhance the happy feeling. Tanhulu has the same effect.

■ 糖葫蘆讓我聯想到焦糖蘋果。那亮麗的顏色和鮮明的甜味增添了歡樂氣氛，糖葫蘆也有類似的效果。

vivid 生動的
sweetness 甜度

> 聯想到焦糖蘋果

■ However, as tanhulu vendors increase, it seems harder to find the **genuine** ones. The **perfect ratio** of sugar coating and the balance with fruit is a science, it can't be messed up.

■ 然而，雖然現在糖葫蘆小販增加了，感覺卻越來越難找到真正的糖葫蘆。砂糖和水果的比例是項科學，那可不能亂做啊！

genuine 真正的
perfect ratio 完美比例

砂糖和水果的比例是項科學

■ Tanghulu needs to be kept under a certain temperature. If it gets too warm, the **coating** will start to melt and thus creating a **sticky** texture.

■ 糖葫蘆需要被保存在特定的溫度下，如果太熱，外層的糖晶會融化，吃起來就會黏黏的。

coating 外層
sticky 黏黏的

需要被保存在特定的溫度下

■ I love pie that is topped with mashed potato and bean paste. It's different from **shepherd's pie**; it's simpler and **lighter**.

■ 我吃過一種在派上面疊了馬鈴薯泥和豆子泥的肉派，跟牧羊人派相當不同。這種派更單純，對身體較無負擔。

> 這種派更單純，對身體較無負擔

shepherd's pie 牧羊人派
lighter 較無負擔的

■ The three elements of a good meat pie are **properly seasoned beef**, gravy and a **perfect crust**. Any of it fails, start over again!

■ 一個好的肉派需要三個元素：適度調味的牛肉、肉汁和一個完美的派皮。要是其中之一沒達到標準，最好砍掉重練哦！

> 適度調味的牛肉和一個完美的派皮

properly seasoned beef 適度調味的牛肉
perfect crust 完美的派皮

1 生活、娛樂、科技和交通

2 異國飲食和人文風情

3 教育、知識、學習

4 工作和金錢的使用

要具體答好這幾類話題需要事先想好各個細節點，這樣在答起來時才不會有不一致的情況或者是表達時態用錯的情況發生。如果背誦佳句的話，多注意「過去」或「未來」等關鍵詞，因為考官問題一改變時許多時態都需要跟著變化了。

Part

3

抽象類話題❶：
教育、知識、
學習

MP3 056

學習方式－
音樂 ❶

■ Music is quite soothing. Listening to soft music while studying is the key to my **academic** success, and the idea comes from the English teaching theory, **suggestopedia**.

■ 音樂是相當撫慰人心的。念書時聽柔性音樂是我學術成功的關鍵，而這想法來自於英語教學理論中的暗示性教學。

academic 學術的
suggestopedia 暗示性教學

242

- I actually **adapted** it into another form. Listening to foreign music accelerates my **pace** of accommodating into other language settings.

學習方式－
音樂 ❷

- 我實際上將這個方式改編成另一個形式。聽外國音樂加速我適應其他語言環境的步調。

adapt 改編
pace 步調

- I guess the most important thing about studying is to know your learning style first so that you will pick up the **rhythm** really quick and have enough **passion** and confidence to study.

學習方式－
音樂 ❸

- 我想學習中最重要的是首先要知道你的學習型態，你就可以很快掌握其中的韻律而且有足夠的熱情和信心學習。

rhythm 韻律
passion 熱情

學習方式－繪圖 ❶

■ Different drawings. I can visualize the concept from just viewing it, and it's quite effective. In biology, different charts explain relationships among different animals, whereas in history, different charts **elucidate** historical events chronologically.

■ 不同的繪畫。僅靠觀看圖示，我能將概念形象化，而且成效相當好。在生物學，不同的圖形解釋不同動物間的關係，而在歷史課，不同的圖形以時間順序解釋歷史事件。

elucidate 解釋

學習方式－繪圖 ❷

■ I won't have to recite as hard as my classmates. Sometimes they just wonder how I prepare all those tests in less time, and their **bewilderment** increases after I get an exceedingly high SAT score.

■ 我不需要像我同班同學那樣背的很費力。有時候他們會想我是如何在較少時間內準備好所有那些考試，而且他們的困惑，隨著我拿到異常高分的 SAT 分數而增加。

bewilderment 困惑

學習方式－運動 ❶

■ Since exercising releases **endorphins**, I won't have a bad mood studying history and literature, and I pick up lots of vocabularies during morning jogging.

■ 既然運動釋放了腦內啡，我不會在讀歷史和文學時有壞心情，而且我在晨間慢跑時，掌握許多字彙。

endorphin 腦內啡

學習方式－運動 ❷

■ I set a **strict** daily routine for me to study and I structure it. I always do the morning jogging while listening to recorded English course content, and right after the jogging I study history and literature.

■ 我制定了嚴格的日規劃行程來學習並組織它。我總是在做晨間慢跑時聽錄製的英語課程內容，而在慢跑後我研讀歷史和文學。我僅需要在考試前複習一下子。

strict 嚴格的

個人規劃：描述對未來的目標

MP3 057

未來目標－替野生動物募款

❶

■ My goal is to raise money for wild animals. It seems kind of different from the goal everyone would do, but it's **meaningful** and unique in my eye... kind of like the **concept** in Adam Braun's *The Promise of the Pencil*.

■ 我的目標是替野生動物募款。這似乎會與每個人會想要定的目標有所不同，但是在我眼中這是很有意義且獨特的…有點像是亞當‧巴塑的「鉛筆的希望」所提到的概念。

meaningful 有意義的
concept 概念

■ Some wild animals live in a **tortured** life that is just so unbearable. Elephants **get beaten to death** and sloth bears get eaten.

未來目標－替野生動物募款 ❷

■ 有些野生動物過著飽受折磨的生活，令人看了難以忍受。大象被鞭打致死而懶熊被食用。

tortured 折磨的
get beaten to death 被鞭打致死

■ Raising money for them will turn their lives around and hopefully **raise** the **awareness** of hardships of wild animals.

未來目標－替野生動物募款 ❸

■ 替牠們募款最終扭轉它們的生活而且希望能喚起對於野生動物所處困境的意識。

raise 喚起
awareness 困境

1 生活、娛樂、科技和交通

2 異國飲食和人文風情

3 教育、知識、學習

4 工作和金錢的使用

未來目標－存
一百萬美金
❶

■ In Taiwan, you can **frequently** hear people's goal in life is to save a million NT dollars. Mine is to save a million US dollars, which is about 30 times that of most people.

■ 在台灣，你可以常聽到人們的人生的目標是存一百萬台幣。我的話則是存一百萬美元，也就是大概大多數人目標的 30 倍左右。

frequently 頻繁地

未來目標－存
一百萬美金
❷

■ To me, dreaming big is very important, and the money saved **has a total say** in your later life, and how quick you reach that point will **determine** how successful you are in your later life.

■ 對我而言，將夢想做大很重要，而且所存的金錢對於你往後的生活有著絕對的決定權，還有你多快達到那個目標會決定你往後生或能有多成功。

has a total say 有著絕對的決定權
determine 決定

未來目標－創業 ❶

■ My answer is to start my own company. You don't need to have an MBA to know that a **fixed** income **won't get you anywhere**.

■ 我的答案是開創我自己的公司。你不需要有 MBA 才知道固定薪水並不能讓你一展所長。

fixed 固定的
won't get you anywhere 不能讓你一展所長

未來目標－創業 ❷

■ You won't be the kind of the person who sits **comfortably** in the office counting the holiday, and then out of the blue is made **redundant** to the boss.

■ 你不會像是坐在辦公室裡頭數著假期的人那般，而且突然間對於老闆來說是多餘的。

comfortably 舒適地
redundant 多餘的

個人特質：描述對一個人來說最重要的特質

MP3 058

最重要的特
質－高度動機
❶

■ The most important quality is to be highly motivated. Remember that's the **criteria** that HR people use to **assess** a person's ability in the workplace. it's not just your intelligence or your ability.

■ 最重要的特質是有高度動機。記得人事部的人在評估一個人在工作場所能力的標準嗎？不僅僅是你的智力或你的能力。

criteria 標準
assess 評估

■ It's your motivation to the job and your ability. You **multiply** one's **motivation** and one's ability, and then you get what a person will bring to the company.

最重要的特質－高度動機
❷

■ 是關於你對於這份工作的動機和你的能力。你將一個人的動機乘上一個人的能力，然後你就可以得知這個人會替公司帶來什麼效益。

motivation 動機
multiply 乘上

■ A highly motivated person will eventually **outperform** those who rest on their intelligence and **diploma**, but with a little motivation.

最重要的特質－高度動機
❸

■ 具高度動機的人最終會表現超越那些僅仰賴自己本身智力和學歷但卻有著些許動機者。

outperform 超越
diploma 文憑

1 生活、娛樂、科技和交通

2 異國飲食和人文風情

3 教育、知識、學習

4 工作和金錢的使用

最重要的特質－毅力 ❶

■ The most important quality is persistence not because it's something that we are frequently heard like "see **persistence** pays off in the end" but because "nothing in the world can **take the place of** persistence."

■ 最重要的特質是毅力，不是因為有些我們常聽到話語像是「看吧！最終毅力讓結果有所回報」，而是因為「在這世界上沒有任何事物能取代毅力」。

persistence 毅力

最重要的特質－毅力 ❷

■ The latter is actually from Ray Kroc's *Grinding It Out*, and how he gets where he is today and how his story **inspires** many people.

■ 後者實際上是源自於雷‧克洛克的「永不放棄：我如何打造麥當勞王國」，而且他如何贏得現今所有的成就和他的故事激勵許多人。

inspire 激勵

■ Talent, genius, and education won't take the place of persistence. So be persistent so that you will not give up when mounting pressure or whatever **instabilities** come to you.

最重要的特質－毅力 ❸

■ 才能、天賦和教育都不能取代毅力的地位。所以保有毅力這樣你才能在壓力排山倒海而來時或者是事情出現任何變動時，抱持不放棄的態度。

instabilities 不穩定

■ Hard-working is the most important **quality** for a university student, if he or she wants to be successful. People with a **hedonistic** mindset show a less focused attention on the job.

最重要的特質－努力 ❶

■ 努力工作對於一個大學學生來說是最重要的特質，如果他或她想要成功的話。抱持著享樂主義者展現在工作時展現得較不專注。

quality 特質
hedonistic 享樂的

學習成長：談論一位你所欣賞的作家

 MP3 059

■ Clayton M. Christensen, author of *How Will You Measure Your life* is the famous person that I **admire**. Through his book, you can always find something to learn, like **compendium** of wisdom that will be quite helpful for every aspect of your life.

欣賞的作家－
Clayton
❶

■ 克雷頓‧克里斯汀生，「你如何衡量你的人生」的作者是我最欽佩的名人。透過他的書籍，你總是可以找到可以學習的東西，像是濃縮版的智慧寶典，

admire 欽佩
compendium 概要

欣賞的作家－
Clayton
❷

■ No matter how successful you are in life, there are **moments** in life that you just can't figure out at the moment, and reading his books will eventually find something that solves the long-term problem.

■ 不論你在生活中有多成功，總有在某個當下你對有些事情無法理出頭緒，而閱讀他的書籍最終要找到解決問題的長遠辦法。

moment 時刻

■ The famous person that I admire is Tyra Banks. The show *America's Next Top Model* is so great. From every season, you get to learn **wisdom** from this lady, not just modeling advice, but also life experience.

欣賞的名人－
Tyra Banks
❶

■ 我最欽佩的名人是泰拉‧班克絲。全美超模是多麼棒的秀。從每季，你可以從這個女士身上學習到智慧，不僅僅是模特兒的建議，還有生活經驗。

wisdom 智慧

■ People are in desperate need of an inner **compass** because they can be so lost sometimes. Sometimes what she says can actually lead people to think in a certain direction.

欣賞的名人－
Tyra Banks
❷

■ 人們迫切需要心理內部的指南針，因為他們可能在有些時候感到迷失。有時候她所說的話實際上可以將人們導向以某個特定方向思考。

compass 指南針

■ Ray Kroc, the person who built the McDonald's empire, is the person I admire. He is an icon with **traditional** values and wisdom for later generations to learn from.

欣賞的作家－
Ray Kroc ❶

■ 雷・克洛克，一位建造麥當勞帝國的人，是我所欽佩的對象。他是指標性人物，有著傳統價值和智慧讓較後面世代們可以從中學習到很多。

traditional 傳統的

欣賞的作家－Ray Kroc ❷

■ In his **memoir**, it reveals he envisions McDonald's restaurants will be popular all over the country. He still believes he has the chance to succeed at the age of 52, totally having a millionaire mind.

■ 在他的回憶錄中，揭漏了他構想麥當勞餐廳會於全國流行開來。在他 52 歲時，他仍相信自己有機會成功，全然有著百萬富翁的心態。

memoir 回憶錄

欣賞的作家－Ray Kroc ❸

■ His success shows there are **no age limits** when it comes to success. Persistence and **determination** will eventually get you there.

■ 他的成功展示了，當提到成功時，是沒有年紀限制的。毅力和決心最終會使你達到你想要的。

no age limits 年紀限制的
determination 決心

一份特別的禮物：曾收到或贈送給人的最棒的特別禮物

MP3 060

特別的禮物－遊戲武器 **❶**

■ A powerful weapon in the online game. In the **fictional** world, players are also perceived by the weapon you have. People want to team up with the person who **possesses** the powerful weapon and knows how to play the game.

■ 線上遊戲中強大的武器。在虛構世界裡，玩家的價值是由你所擁有的武器來評價的。人們想要與擁有強大武器且知道如何玩遊戲的人組隊。

fictional 虛構的
possess 持有

■ But **accumulating** a **certain** amount of money to buy that takes quite some time.

■ 但是累積到定額的金錢去購買要花費相當多的時間。

accumulate 累積
certain 特定的

> 特別的禮物－遊戲武器 ❷

■ One time I gave my friend a powerful weapon as his **birthday present**. Of course, he wrote something on his Facebook wall "best special gift ever received."

■ 有次我把一個強大的武器給我朋友當作他的生日禮物。當然他在他的臉書牆上寫道：「所收到的最棒的特別禮物」。

birthday 生日
present 禮物

> 特別的禮物－遊戲武器 ❸

1 生活、娛樂、科技和交通

2 異國飲食和人文風情

3 教育、知識、學習

4 工作和金錢的使用

特別的禮物－
祖父母的信
❶

■ The special gift was a letter from my grandparents. It's not so much the letter itself as words of **wisdom** from my grandparents.

■ 特別的禮物是一封我祖父母給的信。與其說是信件本身不如說是我祖父母身上的智慧之語。

wisdom 智慧

特別的禮物－
祖父母的信
❷

■ It was written in cursive writing of course, and looks pretty **tattered**. It's like the **prophecy** of my life in the next two decades, totally looks like the clay tablet in *The Richest Man in Babylon*.

■ 當然是以英文草寫書寫成的,看起來相當殘破。它像是我接下來 20 幾年生活的預言,完全像是在「巴比倫最富有的人」書中的泥土碑。

tattered 殘破的
prophecy 預言

■ The most special gift I gave to my friend is an electronic card of the country **club**. You know how expensive that is, but the gift just stood out from the rest in his **promotion** party.

■ 我給我朋友最特別的禮物是鄉村俱樂部的電子感應卡。你知道它有多昂貴，但是在他升遷派對上，這份禮物從所有禮物中超群絕倫。

特別的禮物－俱樂部電子感應卡 ❶

club 俱樂部
promotion 升遷

■ Since my friend just loves to play golf so much, I bought the **electronic** card of the country club for him so that he can play golf for free.

■ 因為我朋友就是很喜愛玩高爾夫球，我購買了鄉村俱樂部的電子感應卡給他，這樣一來他就能免費玩高爾夫球了。

特別的禮物－俱樂部電子感應卡 ❷

electronic 電子的

1 生活、娛樂、科技和交通

2 異國飲食和人文風情

3 教育、知識、學習

4 工作和金錢的使用

MP3 061

■ Different seats. Assigned seats are just an excuse for teachers to conveniently **do the roll call** and it does not require any effort to **memorize** every student.

課堂一
指定座位 ❶

■ 不同的座位。指定座位只是能便於老師點名的藉口，而且不需要花費任何努力去記所有學生名字。

do the roll call 點名
memorize 記

■ I don't want to sit next to a **weird** person... you know the weird type... I will get so **distracted** that I can't recall what the teacher said during the whole lecture.

■ 我不想坐在奇怪的人旁邊... 你知道的奇怪類型的人... 我會如此分心以至於我沒辦法在整堂課期間回想出老師剛才說了些什麼。

weird 奇怪的
distracted 分心的

課堂－
指定座位 ❷

■ After class, I **carry such a negative mood** when I go home, and have to work extra hard to keep up with other students... totally a nightmare... .

■ 在下課後，我回家時會帶著如此負面的情緒在，而且我必須要更努力才能追趕上其他學生... 真的是個夢魘...。

carry such a negative mood 帶著如此負面的情緒

課堂－
指定座位 ❸

1 生活、娛樂、科技和交通

2 異國飲食和人文風情

3 教育、知識、學習

4 工作和金錢的使用

■ Different seats. I do think people who answer students should sit in **assigned** seats are probably not teachers or they probably haven't seen the movie School of Life.

課堂一
不同的座位
❶

■ 不同的座位。我確實認為回答學生該座指定位置的人,可能本身不是老師或他們可能沒看過「優良教師爭奪戰」這部電影。

assigned 指定的
School of Life 優良教師爭奪戰

■ **See what turns out at the end**, you will probably rethink about this question. The assigned seats are fixed and students are feeling so **rigid**.

課堂一
不同的座位
❷

■ 看最後結果是怎樣,你可能就會重新思考這題的問題了。指定座位是固定的而學生覺得太嚴格了。

see what turns out at the end 看最後結果是怎樣
rigid 嚴格的

■ Assigned seats. Whenever you walk into the classroom, you **quickly shift into the mode** of oh... this is my seat... you don't have to **think too much**.

■ 指定座位。每當你走進教室時，你可以很快地進入模式裡的噢... 這是我的座位... 你不用想太多。

quickly shift into the mode 很快地進入模式裡
think too much 想太多

■ Just don't use that as a way for you to **cheat**... like asking the person you are sitting next to let you **peek** a little during the test... kidding.

■ 只是別將這個方式用來便於自己作弊…像是要求座你隔壁的人，在考試時讓你偷看一些些…開玩笑的啦。

cheat 作弊
peek 偷看

課堂—
指定座位 ❹

課堂—
指定座位 ❺

社交：結交朋友

MP3 062

■ You get to learn from different kinds of friends even though you have to do the **superficial** stuff. You just don't know how sometimes **a nodding acquaintance** can be quite helpful if you are out there looking for your ideal jobs.

交友－
結交各類型的
朋友 ❶

■ 你能從不同類型的朋友中學習，即使你必須要做些表面功夫。你不知道有時候就是這樣的點頭之交，在你想要找你的理想工作時發揮相當大的功用。

superficial 表面的
a nodding acquaintance 點頭之交

交友－
結交各類型的
朋友 ❷

■ People within your circle; however, often can only have **emotional support**, but **have nothing to offer**.

■ 人們自己的圈子裡頭，然而，通常只有著情感支持，但是卻沒什麼能幫上忙的。

emotional support 情感支持
have nothing to offer 沒什麼能幫上忙的

交友－
結交各類型的
朋友 ❸

■ A person I know from the party once introduced me to the industry I've been longing to get into. I eventually get the job even though I have no experiences. From that moment on, I'm sort of like **what the heck**, the more the merrier.

■ 一位我從派對上認識的人有次引介我進了我一直想要進入的產業裡。我最終獲取工作，即使我沒有經驗。從那個時刻起，我有點像是管它的，越多人越熱鬧。

what the heck 管它的

■ Personality types **weigh heavily** on this question. Speaking and hanging out with lots of friends **drains your energy** quite a bit.

■ 個性的類型在這個問題上佔了很重的分配。說話和與許多朋友閒晃榨乾你相當多的能量。

weigh heavily 佔了很重的分配
drain your energy 榨乾你的能量

■ It's my free time, and spend some **quality time** with some of your besties and have drinks. You don't have to spend so much time **engaging in idle gossip**, and doing superficial stuff.

■ 這是我的空閒時間，而花些品質時間與一些你的閨密相聚和喝幾杯。你不會需要花費許多時間在聊閒話八卦和做一些表面功夫的東西。

quality time 品質時間
engaging in idle gossip 在聊閒話八卦

交友－
結交各類型的
朋友 ❹

■ I love my **close friends**, but sometimes they just bore me in a certain way. Sometimes I want to **yell** stop already.

■ 我喜愛我的親密朋友，但有時候他們某些程度上只是讓我感到無聊。有時候我想要大叫，快停止啊！

close friends 親密朋友
yell 大叫

交友－
結交各類型的
朋友 ❺

■ With a wide variety of friends, I can often **shift my attention** to something novel... like wow you bought yourself a car... or since when... you are raising a **chameleon**, seriously?

■ 有著各式各樣的朋友時，我通常可以將我的專注力放在一些新奇的事情上... 像是哇你替你自己買了一台車嗎... 或是是什麼時候的事... 你在養變色龍，是真的嗎？

shift my attention 轉移注意力
chameleon 變色龍

Part 4 提供了許多鉅細靡遺的工作類表達，如果不具工作經驗者，可以以書籍中提供的餐飲相關工作經驗為輔助，修正較含糊地表達，講出具體的高分回答。而具工作經驗者也能從中學習更多高分表達句，一舉拿下高分。

抽象類話題❷：
工作和金錢的
使用

MP3 063

■ Well, I'm not very comfortable with the **customers**. I mean, I can cook for them, I can run the business, but talking to the customers **face to face** is not my cup of tea.

招待客戶 ─ 面對面聊天

■ 我對接待客人不是很在行。我是說,我可以為他們做餐點,我也可以經營一家店,但跟客人面對面聊天真的非我所長。

customer 客人
face to face 面對面

招待客戶－熱情待客很重要

■ Being **hospitable** is big. No matter how bad you feel, the moment the customers step through the **threshold**, you have to put away your private feelings and start smiling. It's something against human nature, but it's indispensable.

■ 熱情待客很重要。不論你的心情多憂鬱，在客人踏進店門的霎那，你必須全部拋諸腦後，並綻出微笑。這是違反人性的事，但非做不可。

hospitable 好客的
threshold 門檻

招待客戶－讓人們覺得舒適

■ I'm born to be a server, I feel. I'm always in a good mood and I want to make people feel **cozy** and laid back.

■ 我覺得我生來就是當服務生的料，我的心情總是很好，而且我想讓人們覺得舒適、放鬆。

cozy 舒適的

■ Just **picture** yourself walking into a restaurant. Would you like to see a **cold stiff face**? No! So that's what I tell myself, and I nail it every time.

招待客戶－避免冷冰冰的臉孔

■ 想像你走進一家餐廳,你會想看到冷冰冰的臉孔嗎?當然不!我都是這麼告訴自己的,而每次我總是做得很成功。

picture 想像
cold stiff face (臉)冷若冰霜

■ Every **skill** needs to be trained, so does being a server. If one is **unfamiliar** with serving people, no doubt one is going to have a hard time.

招待客戶－需要訓練

■ 凡事都需要訓練,當服務生也一樣。如果一個人對服務別人不熟悉,不用説,他會過得很辛苦。

skill 技術
unfamiliar 不熟悉的

■ Keen **observation** is fundamental; diligence and **hospitality** are also top priorities. Never be afraid to communicate. Unless one faces the problem, it can't be coped with.

餐間服務－
敏銳的觀察

■ 敏銳的觀察是最基本的，勤奮和好客的態度也很重要。永遠不要擔心和人溝通，除非你正視問題，否則無法解決問題。

observation 觀察
hospitality 好客

■ The **knack** is to enjoy what you do. Try to think in other people's shoes. When serving our diners, I want them to have the best dining experience possible. That is so **important**.

餐間服務－
樂於所做

■ 訣竅在於樂於所做，試著用同理心去對待別人。當我在服務客人時，我希望他們能擁有最棒的用餐經驗。

knack 竅門
important 重要的

Unit 64 介紹餐點、點餐和上餐

介紹餐點－
主餐收益較高

■ I always start from the entrées. Not only that it's more **profit** for us, but also every dish is my pride and joy. **Appetizers** and desserts have their reason to exist, but they are not my focus.

■ 我總是先從主餐開始介紹。不只是因為主餐收益較高，也因為每道菜都是我的驕傲。開胃菜和甜點當然也有存在的必要，但並非我的重點。

profit 利潤
appetizers 開胃菜

介紹餐點－
從銷路最好的

■ The priority does matter. Since there are many items on the menu, it's impossible to introduce every dish, which means that we have to **omit** some items in the introduction. I often start from our best-sellers.

■ 順序當然有影響，因為菜單上品項很多，不可能一一介紹，因此有些菜不會被介紹到。我總是從銷路最好的料理開始介紹。

omit 遺漏掉

點餐－
需要一本小記
事本

■ You will need a note pad with you while taking orders. For instance, if someone wants **meatloaf** without **ketchup** and another wants extra caramelized onions, things might get confused easily.

■ 點餐時，你會需要一本小記事本。舉例來說，如果有人點了肉派不加番茄醬，另一個人點肉派和特多焦糖洋蔥，這很容易搞混。

meatloaf 肉派
ketchup 番茄醬

■ I once brought a plate of hash browns with **Hungarian meat sauce** instead of cream of **mushroom** to a customer. For her, it was a big problem because she was a vegetarian.

■ 有一次，我本應給客人蘑菇白醬炸薯餅，卻拿成匈牙利肉醬炸薯餅。對她來説，這是個很大的冒犯，因為她是素食主義者。

Hungarian meat sauce 匈牙利肉醬
mushroom 蘑菇

■ and I **guaranteed** her that we had a vegan hash brown combo. It was a **catastrophe**. Since then, I take extra caution while taking orders.

■ 而我向她保證我們提供素食炸薯餅套餐。那是個災難。自從那次起，我總是在點餐時格外留心。

guarantee 保證
catastrophe 災難

- I still jump up on my toes when I hear the kitchen cry out "order up". It's like **magic** words that make me **instantly** run in there to take the food.

上餐－
廚房大喊
「上菜！」

- 直到現在，當廚房大喊「上菜！」時，我還是會立刻跳起來。那些字眼就像魔法般帶著我即刻衝進廚房拿餐點。

magic 魔法的
instantly 立即地

- It's an exciting moment when the food is **piping hot**, **smelling heavenly**, and ready to be delivered to the empty stomachs waiting for it. I don't know if I'll ever get tired of it.

上餐－
工作熱情

- 那個餐點熱騰騰、香氣四溢、準備被送進空洞的胃袋的時刻很讓人興奮。我覺得我永不會對這項工作感到厭煩。

piping hot 熱氣蒸騰的
smelling heavenly 香氣四溢

訂位、預先點餐、外帶餐點

MP3 065

■ Name and phone number are the basic **requirements** for these occasions. The groups often have **expectations** for certain seats, such as a four-person family wanting a corner table or a two-person group wanting sofa seats.

預先點餐－
基本的資訊

■ 客人的姓名和電話號碼是訂位時最基本的資訊。通常客人都會自己選定座位，例如四人小家庭或情侶兩人，就可能會要沙發座或角落的桌次等。

requirement 要求
expectation 期待

■ If the guests don't show up at the **scheduled** hour, we have **a ten-minute policy** of holding their seats open. No longer than that.

預先點餐－
留位十分鐘的
政策

■ 如果客人沒有依約定的時間出現，我們有留位十分鐘的政策，時間超過就不再保留了。

scheduled 表定的
a ten-minute policy 十分鐘的政策

■ **Pickup ordering** is a big business and it's popular among folks. I was afraid of **hoax calls** but things have turned out to be great so far.

外帶點餐－
惡作劇點餐電
話

■ 外帶點餐是個很大的商機，人們也喜歡。我本來很擔心會有惡作劇點餐電話，但到目前為止還沒發生過。

Pickup ordering 外帶點餐
hoax calls 惡作劇點餐電話

■ Usually, the **takeout box** is sealed in the last minutes of preparing an order to prevent the loss of certain textures in the food. I don't want the guest picking up our fried chicken and it's **soggy** already.

外帶點餐－避免食材喪失口感

■ 通常外帶盒是在最後一刻才密封，這樣能避免一些食材喪失口感。我可不想要客人外帶炸雞，卻發現麵衣已經濕軟了。

takeout box 外帶盒
soggy 濕軟的

■ On average, a pickup order takes about 25 minutes. You want to help the customers **arrive** on time so the food is **fresh** and hot.

外帶點餐－須等二十五分鐘

■ 平均而言，外帶點餐須等二十五分鐘。你會希望客人抵達的時候食物剛好做好，還是熱騰騰的。

arrive 抵達
fresh 新鮮的

預先點餐－
有長者或孩子
同行

■ Well, I don't see it as such a bad thing. If the customer is taking **seniors** or young children with them, they might want to **shorten** the waiting time.

■ 我覺得這不是件壞事。如果客人有長者或孩子同行，他們可能不想等那麼久。

senior 年長者
shorten 縮短

預先點餐－
可以在電話中
直接點餐

■ I **understand** it, so sometimes I'd tell them that they can **order** on the phone. My bosses don't quite like it, though.

■ 我了解這點，所以有時候我會告訴他們，可以在電話中直接點餐。我的老闆們不喜歡我這麼做就是了。

understand 了解
order 點餐

■ If I'm able to, I surely will. Most of the customers are polite and **considerate**. They don't get upset if their needs are **rejected**. Instead, they feel sorry about it.

客製化餐點—
會接受

■ 能力所及的話,我當然會接受。大多數的客人都有禮且體貼,他們不會因自己的要求被拒而惱羞成怒。相反的,他們會覺得不好意思。

considerate 體貼的
rejected 拒絕的

Removing eggs, dairy and **nuts** isn't a big thing to me, and that's pretty much what they want most of the time.

客製化餐點－不要雞蛋、奶製品和堅果

■ 不要雞蛋、奶製品和堅果對我來説輕而易舉，而多數時候客人的要求就是這些而已。

remove 移除
nuts 堅果

I will leave some room for **negotiation**. For instance, if there is a football game going, I will let the **enthusiastic** guests stay as long as the game goes.

營業時間－橄欖球賽

■ 我認為這有討論的空間。舉例來説，如果當天有橄欖球賽，我會讓那些激昂的客人們待到比賽結束。

negotiation 協商
enthusiastic 熱情的

1 生活、娛樂、科技和交通

2 異國飲食和人文風情

3 教育、知識、學習

4 工作和金錢的使用

- Closing the door on time is **ideal**, but technically speaking, this idea doesn't always bring in more **profits**.

- 準時關店雖然理想，但以技術層面來說，這個概念無法帶來更多收益。

ideal 理想的
profit 利益

- Working in a restaurant, you always have **extra** work to do. Sometimes we even **receive** orders when we're about to close. All these pots and pans are killing me.

- 在餐廳工作永遠有做不完的事，有時候我們甚至在關店前收到顧客點餐。清洗這些鍋碗瓢盆真是累壞我了。

extra 額外的
receive 接受

1 生活、娛樂、科技和交通

營業時間－
我不是老闆

■ **Frankly**, since I'm not the owner, I'd rather get off duty **on time**, although this never happens.

■ 坦白說，因為我不是老闆，我寧可準時下班，雖然這種事情從未發生過。

Frankly 坦白說
on time 準時

2 異國飲食和人文風情

營業時間－
嚴格規定時間
較好

■ **Strict** business hours are much better for employees. In fact, it's better for everyone except the **customers**.

■ 嚴格規定營業時間對員工來說比較好。事實上，對每個人都比較好，顧客除外。

Strict 嚴格的
customers 顧客

3 教育、知識、學習

4 工作和金錢的使用

287

■ **Vegetarianism** is a growing trend. A successful restaurant must have vegetarian meals. In my place, I train the staff to talk to our diners as much as possible, so we can understand their needs and offer **proper** food.

素食餐點—是個趨勢

■ 素食族群是個成長中的趨勢，一間成功的餐廳必須提供素食餐點。在我的店裡，我訓練員工盡量多跟客人溝通，了解他們的需求，我們才能提供合適的餐點。

Vegetarianism 素食主義
proper 適當的

■ It's not impossible to make a vegan meal out of an **ordinary** dish. The problem is if we are asked to modify our **recipes**, the texture of the food might not be the same.

素食餐點－要求更動食譜

■ 將一般料理轉變為素食料理並非不可能，問題在於，當我們被要求更動食譜時，料理的口感可能會變得不一樣。

ordinary 普遍的
recipe 食譜

■ We always want our guests to **understand** this, and understand that we are willing to **provide** what they want.

素食餐點－樂意調製他們想要的

■ 我們總是盡力讓客人了解這點，並讓他們知道我們很樂意調製他們想要的餐點。

understand 了解
provide 提供

攜帶寵物一
食安問題

- Animals are not **suitable** in our diner or in most diners. It's a matter of food sanitation. Supposed that some dogs and cats have not been **vaccinated**?

- 寵物跟我們餐廳格格不入，或許對大部分餐廳都是如此。這是食安問題。若是有些貓狗沒有預防注射怎麼辦？

suitable 合適的
vaccinate 注射疫苗

攜帶寵物一
其他怪要求
也隨之而來

- Moreover, if we **accept** cats and dogs, should we accept birds, frogs, goats and **snakes**?

- 再說，如果我們接納貓狗，我們是不是也要接納鳥、青蛙、山羊和蛇？

accept 接納
snake 蛇

■ I'm a mom myself, so I'm all for a family to dine in my restaurant. Kids are **unpredictable**, they are like bombs that will **ignite** when you least expect it.

> 帶兒童前往－
> 孩子們很難控制

■ 我自己是個母親，所以我非常贊成一家子到我的餐廳用餐。孩子們很難控制，他們就像炸彈一樣，會在你沒有警覺的時候引爆。

unpredictable 無法預測的
ignite 引爆

■ For this reason, we have a whole set of kid's tableware and infant chairs. It's a joy to see families dining together, and it's our duty to provide a convivial **ambience**.

> 帶兒童前往－
> 提供一個歡樂
> 的用餐氣氛

■ 因為這緣故，我們購置了整套的兒童餐具以及嬰兒座椅。看家人在一起用餐令人快樂，而我們的責任就是提供一個歡樂的用餐氣氛。

ambience 氣氛

MP3 068

生日驚喜派
對－點更多食
物和飲料

- True that some people get too excited with their **celebration**, and they **disturb** other diners. But most of the time, people behave themselves, and they order a lot of food and drinks for the event.

- 的確，有的人會在慶生的時候太興奮，以至於影響到其他顧客。但大多時候，人們還是很守規矩的，而且他們會因為特別活動而點更多食物和飲料。

celebration 慶祝
disturb 打擾

生日驚喜派
對－噩夢一場

■ It's a kitchen **nightmare** to have 20 tickets pouring in all of a sudden. Whenever we have a party **reservation** like that, it's always nerve-racking.

■ 二十張點單一時之間湧入廚房，簡直是噩夢一場。當有人來餐廳辦派對之類的活動的時候，我總是如坐針氈。

nightmare 夢魘
reservation 預訂

生日驚喜派對－
為壽星獻唱德文
的生日快樂歌

■ One time, I offered to sing the happy birthday song in German and it was a big hit. I like to make people happy, in short. Plus, the bonus is usually good: a **generous** tip!

■ 有一次，我為壽星獻唱德文的生日快樂歌，結果大得迴響。總之，我喜歡讓別人開心，而且，附加價值也高，也就是會得到很多小費！

generous 慷慨的

■ Try not to make any mistakes, that's the first priority. We are a **popular** restaurant so we are **crowded** at lunch time.

■ 試著別犯錯，這是第一要務。我們餐廳很熱門，午餐時間總是相當忙碌。

popular 熱門的
crowded 擁擠的

■ There is no time to **fix** somebody's steak or do an eggs benedict over again. I always feel my nerve, because **the devil is in the details**.

■ 我不會有時間去處理客人的牛排問題，或重作一份班尼迪克蛋。我總是戰戰兢兢，因為魔鬼藏在細節裡。

fix 修復
the devil is in the details 魔鬼藏在細節裡

■ If it's not a serious error, such as having made squid instead of **shrimp**, I may just tell them that the **squid** is fresher and see if they want squid instead.

做錯餐點－把蝦子做成墨魚

■ 如果錯誤不嚴重，例如把蝦子做成墨魚，我可能會告訴客人墨魚比較新鮮，看他們要不要換點墨魚。

shrimp 蝦
squid 墨魚

■ When I'm in charge, I won't let those kinds of mistake **pass through**. Every ticket needs to be cared for, even in the **busiest** hour. It's all about experience, I will say.

做錯餐點－這跟經驗有關

■ 當我在廚房坐鎮時，我不會讓這種錯誤過關。每張點單都必須留意，就算在最忙的時候也一樣。這跟經驗有關。

pass through 通過；過關
busiest 最忙的

料理細節、更換餐點和食材用光

 MP3 069

■ Every **food-related** problem that happens in my place is a shame, even if we are not the cause. I always train my **employees** to ask our diners if they have any conditions like that.

> 料理細節
> 有疑慮－
> 主動詢問客人

■ 在我的餐廳裡發生任何跟食物有關的問題，不管是否肇因於我們，都是一件負面的事。我總是訓練員工主動詢問客人，看他們是否有任何這方面的問題。

food-related 食物有關的
employee 員工

■ The question most commonly asked is if the food contains eggs. So many people are allergic to eggs, yet egg is a crucial binding ingredient for **meatballs**, burger patties, and **pancakes** to name a few.

料理細節有疑慮－食物裡是否含蛋

■ 詢問度最高的問題是食物裡是否含蛋。太多人對蛋過敏，可是蛋卻是肉丸、漢堡排和鬆餅等料理中的重要連結原料。

meatball 肉丸
pancake 鬆餅

■ So, we wrote it on the menu that if anyone needs an **eggless** meal, to please **inform** the server. This saves tons of work.

料理細節有疑慮－請告知服務生

■ 因此，我們就直接在菜單上標示，若有人需要無蛋料理，請告知服務生。這給我們省下不少功夫。

eggless 無蛋的
inform 告知

1
生活、娛樂、科技和交通

2
異國飲食和人文風情

3
教育、知識、學習

4
工作和金錢的使用

■ It's not **pleasant**, but I'll make the change. For me, the **satisfaction** of the diners is the first thing that I care about.

■ 這不太令人愉快，但我會做更動。對我來說，顧客滿意度是我最關心的事。

pleasant 令人愉悅的
satisfaction 滿意

■ I'm not the one that makes the food, so I'm probably not that **annoyed**. However, I'm not **thrilled** to pass on this message to the kitchen.

■ 我不是煮飯的那個人，所以被惹惱的程度比較低。不過，要把這類訊息傳達給廚房，我也是不太樂意的。

annoyed 惱人的
thrilled 非常高興的

食材用完－常發生配菜不足

■ Quite frequently, what we run out of is the **side dishes**. Bok choy, **baby spinach**, coleslaw, etc.

■ 很常發生配菜不足的情況，例如青江菜、幼菠菜葉或涼拌捲心菜等。

side dishes 配菜
baby spinach 幼菠菜葉

■ We still need them to accomplish our main course, so I'm trained to move very fast. Take **coleslaw** for example, I'll use a cheese grater to quickly **shave up** a cabbage and whip it up.

食材用完－用起司刨刀

■ 我們還是需要這些配菜來完成整道主菜，因此我的動作被訓練得越來越快。舉涼拌捲心菜為例，我會用起司刨刀很快地削完一顆高麗菜，然後做出涼拌捲心菜來。

coleslaw 涼拌捲心菜
shave up 削（蔬菜）

MP3 070

打破餐具—
可能會被解僱

■ First of all, it makes a difference whether our employees or the customers broke the **tableware**. If our servers broke it, depending on the frequency and the level of the loss, I have to decide one's **eligibility**.

■ 首先，要看是員工打破東西，還是顧客，這有所不同。如果是服務生打破的，依照頻繁度和損失程度，我必須決定其去留。

tableware 餐具
eligibility 適任性

打破餐具－
小孩改給塑膠
餐具

■ Replacing broken glasses isn't so bad; what gives me a big **headache** is cleaning up the spilled liquid, sometimes hot soup. Young kids will definitely need **plastic** tableware.

■ 換上新的玻璃杯不是難事，讓我頭大的是清理潑出來的液體或熱湯。小孩子絕對需要塑膠餐具。

headache 頭痛
plastic 塑膠的

送錯桌－
嚴重缺失

■ If I were the diner, I would see this restaurant as an **unorganized**, **disastrous** place if the food came to the wrong table. This is a serious matter.

■ 如果我是顧客，我會覺得一間餐點送錯桌的店家不嚴謹、沒有員工訓練。這是個嚴重的問題。

unorganized 雜亂的
disastrous 災難的

送錯桌－
可能重創生意

■ You never know who you are serving the food to, and a **displeased** food critic can really **hurt** the business.

■ 你永遠不知道你送餐的對象是誰，而一則負面美食評論可是能重創我們的生意呢。

displeased 不開心的
hurt 傷害

食材短缺－
餐廳的印象變
差

■ If we just blind them and tell them to wait for an **uncertain** amount of time, not only they are not promised to get the food, but also they will have poor experience dining in our **restaurant**.

■ 如果我們呼攏客人，告訴他們必須等，但不告訴他們要等多久，這不僅對客人沒保障，說不定還會讓他們對我們餐廳的印象變差。

uncertain 不確定的
restaurant 餐廳

食材短缺－誠實告知

■ I **figure** that telling them we are out of food and suggesting other options may be a **wiser** thing to do.

■ 我發現最好的方法是誠實告知食材售完，並建議客人點別道菜。

figure 發現
wiser 較明智的

食材短缺－不可拒絕客人的點餐

■ There's no way that we're gonna tell and return the tickets. Even though we are **running out** of food, we don't **turn** the customers **down**.

■ 絕不可以拒絕客人的點餐。就算食材真的售罄，我們也不會取消點單。

run out 用完
turn down 拒絕

■ I can't agree with you more. One of the most fatal problems in the kitchen is to prepare the food with **unclean** hands. Hairs, blood, and nail polish are **strictly** prohibited in the kitchen.

廚房食安－注意頭髮、血液、指甲油

■ 我非常同意。廚房裡最致命的問題之一，就是用不乾淨的手料理食材。頭髮、血液、指甲油在廚房裡都是嚴格禁止的。

unclean 不潔的
strictly 嚴格地

■ We don't want to serve food that **contains** these items, do we? Healthy food is our **promise** to the customers.

廚房食安－
對顧客的承諾

■ 我們不希望我們提供的食物裡混雜這些東西，對吧？健康的料理是我們對顧客的承諾。

contain 包含
promise 承諾

■ Never, ever use bare hands to touch the ingredients when there's a wound. Whether it's a deep cut or not, **bleeding** or not, there are invisible **germs** invading and polluting everything that contacts it.

廚房食安－
避免赤手調理
食物

■ 手上有傷口的話，千萬不可以赤手調理食物。不論傷口大或小、是否流血，無形的細菌都會沾染並汙染所有觸摸到的東西。

bleeding 流血
germ 細菌

1 生活、娛樂、科技和交通

2 異國飲食和人文風情

3 教育、知識、學習

4 工作和金錢的使用

305

■ It's literally a matter of life or death. Food **contamination** is so **crucial** yet so easy to be neglected. Working in this industry is all about one's heart.

■ 這是名副其實的生死攸關之事。食品汙染非同小可,但卻容易受到忽視。在這個產業工作,最重要的就是個人的良心。

contamination 汙染
crucial 關鍵的

■ I always go in the kitchen three or four hours before service out of fear that this **situation** will take place. If it does, I will prepare the **ingredients** ASAP.

■ 我總是提早三、四小時進廚房,就是怕有這種情況發生。如果真的發生了,我會盡快準備食材。

situation 狀況
ingredient 食材

■ For instance, if the meat is still frozen, I'll thaw it in the **microwave**. But if the stock is not enough, I **suppose** that I will have to be prepared to be cooked.

食材處理－
丟到微波爐裡
解凍

■ 例如，如果肉還是冷凍的，我會丟到微波爐裡解凍。但如果高湯煮不夠，我想我會準備好被老闆電。

microwave 微波爐
suppose 認為

■ I mean, the **loss** is not on me if something's not ready to be sold today. Still, I have to solve the problem, and the **secret** is to move really fast.

食材處理－動
作快

■ 我是說，如果有東西沒準備好，當天不能賣，損失也不是算在我頭上。不過，我還是得解決問題，而秘訣是動作快！

loss 損失
secret 秘訣

1 生活、娛樂、科技和交通

2 異國飲食和人文風情

3 教育、知識、學習

4 工作和金錢的使用

工作求職：求職時的面試建議

MP3 072

■ You also need to study **intensely** about the corporate cultures and prepare at least five questions you would like to ask after the **interviewer** asks you do you have any questions?

求職面試－
準備問題

■ 你也需要深入研究公司文化和至少準備五個問題，在面試官詢問你「你還有任何問題嗎？」時，可以問對方。

intensely 強烈地
interviewer 面試官

求職面試－衣著和外貌乾淨

- Buying yourself a **decent** suit and making you look like a **clean-cut** person are just a part of it.

- 買個像樣的西裝而且讓你自己看起來乾乾淨淨的僅是準備的一部分。

decent 體面的
clean-cut 整潔好看的

求職面試－Knock'em Dead ❶

- *Knock'em Dead*, of course, it like the basic before going to an interview. I just can't **imagine** why some people go to an interview without **preparing** interview questions from *Knock'em Dead*.

- 當然是 *Knock'em Dead* 啊，這像是參加面試前的基本準備。我真的無法想像有些人去參加面試，絲毫無準備 *Knock'em Dead* 裡的面試問題。

imagine 想像
prepare 準備

1 生活、娛樂、科技和交通

2 異國飲食和人文風情

3 教育、知識、學習

4 工作和金錢的使用

■ Often you can **blow** the chance for your desired job and **regret** from ten years on that I wish I had prepared those questions.

■ 通常你會搞砸你想要的工作機會，而十年後後悔著但願我當時有準備那些問題。

blow 搞砸
regret 後悔

■ Good **eye contact**. Definitely the most important one. Most of **human interactions** rest on good eye contact.

■ 良好的眼神接觸。絕對是最重要的一個。大多數人類互動是仰賴良好的眼神接觸。

eye contact 眼神接觸
human interactions 人類互動

■ Interviewers are looking at you to see if you are **confident** enough, or **whether** you are certain about the thing you just said.

求職面試－眼神接觸 ❷

■ 面試者注視著你檢視著你是否有足夠的自信或是你是否很確定你自己所講述的話。

confident 自信的
whether 是否

■ Or whether you are telling them the truth, and sometimes trust comes from having good eye contact. From my experience as an HR **manager**, interviewees who maintain good eye contact generally leave a good **impression**.

求職面試－眼神接觸 ❸

■ 或你是否是講實話，而有時候信賴來自於良好的眼神接觸。從我當人事經理的經驗，面試者們能維持良好的眼神接觸，一般來說都能留下良好的印象。

manager 經理
impression 印象

MP3 073

未來想從事工
作－巧克力或
啤酒品嚐員❶

■ The special job I would like to do in the future is a taste **tester** at a **brewery** or a chocolate plant. Someone actually pays you to eat or drink. I don't think any job can compete with it.

■ 在未來我想要從事的特別工作是巧克力或啤酒品嚐員。有人實際上付你錢要你吃或喝東西。我不認為任何工作能與之相比。

tester 試驗員
brewery 啤酒廠

■ Taking eating chocolate for example, you get to eat different kinds and some are **decorated** with **fancy** decorations. You can eat them before they are on the market.

■ 以巧克力品嚐員為例，你能夠吃各式不同種類的，而且有些巧克力還以豪華方式裝飾。你可以在上市前就吃到它們。

decorate 裝飾
fancy 豪華的

未來想從事工作－巧克力或啤酒品嚐員❷

■ The special job I would like to do in the future is the **island** guard. Places on the island will be decorated like holiday **resorts**, and I love beach and enjoy sunshine.

■ 未來我想要從事的特別工作是島嶼看守員。島上的地方會被裝飾成像渡假勝地般，而且我喜愛海灘和享受陽光。

island 島嶼
resort 渡假勝地

未來想從事工作－島嶼看守員❶

■ This motivates a lot simply because every morning when you are awake, you get to see beautiful scenery out there. You just need to do what you love so that you have the **impetus** to motivate you to wake up.

■ 這大大地驅策著我因為每個早晨當你醒來，你能夠看到外頭的美麗景色。你就是需要從事你喜愛的工作，這樣一來你才會有動力驅策你起床。

impetus 動力

■ The special job I would like to do in the future is be a cartoon writer. What's more fun than being a cartoon writer? You **fabricate** some stories and you're done for the day.

■ 在未來我想要從事的特別工作是卡通寫作者。還能有比當卡通寫作者好玩的工作了嗎？你編造一些故事，然後你今天就到這為止了。

fabricate 編造

■ Once in a while, the company sends you to several **amazing** places for you to study how animals behave so that you can **depict** certain animals more specifically.

未來想從事
工作－卡通寫
作者 ❷

■ 偶爾，公司會送你到幾個令人感到驚奇的地方去研究下動物如何展示其行為，如此一來你就能夠更確切地描繪出特定的動物。

amazing 驚奇的
depict 描繪

■ You get to enjoy yourself during all these trips and learn and it **boosts your creativity** in some ways. You will get more ideas in some **exotic** places.

未來想從事
工作－卡通寫
作者 ❸

■ 你可以在這些假期時自我享受一下並學習，而這些都能在某種程度上增進你的創意。你會在一些異國風情的地方有更多想法。

boost your creativity 提升你的創意
exotic 異國情調的

1 生活、娛樂、科技和交通

2 異國飲食和人文風情

3 教育、知識、學習

4 工作和金錢的使用

金錢、消費習慣和理財：該將額外的錢花掉還是存起來

MP3 074

金錢和理財—
存錢 ❶

■ Save the extra money. I'm an advocate of living your life to the fullest, and like everyone once in a while I do **indulge** myself with a little shopping and **international** trips.

■ 存下額外的錢。我是主張人該盡其所能享受自己的人生者，而且像每個人一樣偶爾我也會縱容自己有些購物和去國際旅行。

indulge 縱容
international 國際的

■ But that money is not from my **payment**, my fixed income. It's from the house rent every month I receive, and you can't spend your fixed income on luxuries and international trips.

■ 但是那些金錢不是來自於我的薪資，我固定的收入。而是來自於每個月我所收到的租金，你就是不能使用你的固定收入花費在奢侈品和國際旅遊上。

payment 薪資

■ You can only use your bonuses, investment money from the stock market, or house rent you receive on leisure activities or for pleasure. So saving money… till you have the **capability** to enjoy the fruit of it.

■ 你僅能使用你的獎金、從股市投資賺來的錢、或是你所收到的房租來從事休閒活動或得到樂趣。所以存錢吧…直到你有能力享用存錢後所帶來的果實。

capability 能力

金錢和理財－存錢 ❷

金錢和理財－存錢 ❸

1 生活、娛樂、科技和交通

2 異國飲食和人文風情

3 教育、知識、學習

4 工作和金錢的使用

■ Of course, the **answer** is to save the extra money. Remember the old **wisdom** from *The Richest Man in Babylon*, money comes to those who save it.

■ 當然，答案是存下額外的錢。記得「巴比倫最富有的人」裡頭的古老智慧嗎？，金錢來自於那些將它存下者。

answer 答案
wisdom 智慧

金錢和理財－
存錢 ❹

■ **Frittering** away with the money can only give you the **transient** pleasure, but once the excitement goes away, you are right back to where you are.

■ 揮霍浪費掉金錢只會使你獲得短暫的樂趣，但是一旦那種興奮感消逝，你馬上回到本來的狀態。

fritter 揮霍浪費
transient 短暫的

金錢和理財－
存錢 ❺

金錢和理財－花光錢 ❶

■ Why can't I just spend all the extra money... and to be honest, **saving for the rainy day** thing is an old concept…you just have to **let go of it**.

■ 為什麼我不能花掉所有額外的金錢呢... 而且說實話，未雨綢繆是老舊的觀點了... 你本該放掉這個觀點。

saving for the rainy day 未雨綢繆
let go of it 捨棄掉

金錢和理財－花光錢 ❷

■ In life, you can't even know what's going to happen to you in the next **second**. No one knows... even the **fortune-teller** does not.

■ 在生命中，你甚至無法得知下一秒會發生什麼事。沒有人知道... 甚至算命師都不知道。

second 秒
fortune-teller 算命師

國家圖書館出版品預行編目(CIP)資料

一次就考到雅思口說7+ / Amanda Chou著--
初版. -- 新北市：倍斯特, 2019.06面 ; 公分.--
（考用英語系列 ; 017）
ISBN 978-986-97075-7-2（平裝附光碟）
1.國際英語語文測試系統　2.考試指南

805.189　　　　　　　　　　　　108007684

考用英語系列　017

一次就考到雅思口說7⁺（附英式發音MP3）

初　　版　　2019年6月
定　　價　　新台幣460元

作　　者　　Amanda Chou
出　　版　　倍斯特出版事業有限公司
發 行 人　　周瑞德
電　　話　　886-2-8245-6905
傳　　真　　886-2-2245-6398
地　　址　　23558 新北市中和區立業路83巷7號4樓
E - m a i l　　best.books.service@gmail.com
官　　網　　www.bestbookstw.com
總 編 輯　　齊心瑀
企劃編輯　　陳韋佑
封面構成　　高鍾琪
內頁構成　　菩薩蠻數位文化有限公司
印　　製　　大亞彩色印刷製版股份有限公司

港澳地區總經銷　　泛華發行代理有限公司
地　　址　　香港新界將軍澳工業邨駿昌街7號2樓
電　　話　　852-2798-2323
傳　　真　　852-3181-3973